Beauty Fierce as Stars:

And Other Science-Fiction Tales of Mystery and Intrigue

Beauty Fierce as Stars:

And Other Science-Fiction Tales of Mystery and Intrigue

JEREMY BALFOUR

TENTH STREET PRESS

THIS EDITION

© Copyright 2013 Jeremy Balfour

Published by Tenth Street Press   2013

Front cover image taken from the oil painting *Beauty Trap (copulating sparrows)*
By Charles Browning 2011, used with kind permission
Design by Tenth Street Press

ISBN: 0-9923034-4-3
ISBN13: 978-0-9923034-4-0

PRINTED IN U.S.A.

TENTH STREET PRESS Ltd.
MELBOURNE LONDON
www.tenthstreetpress.com
Email:contact@tenthstreetpress.com

Jeremy Balfour

Contents

CHAPTER ONE:
Caligula the Mad

Pluto was the gateway to the underworld, Sir Arthur Eddington well knew. The space ladder lead him up to the Extra-Large Particle Accelerator which encircled the solar system. He approached with great trepidation the final moment of his project, even as far away the earth was about to be destroyed. But he knew he was right: the only way to prevent the great holocaust was to make time move backwards. Yet was this a fate worse still? This he could not predict.

In the Pentagon's secret briefing chamber, General Waldheim was about to press a red button, and once and for all end the Cold War with Canada.

Arthur Eddington reached the Large Array and pointed up in his suit, his left eye twitching with a nervous tic, and pressed a green button. At least World War III was prevented.

He descended the ladder with alacrity, to go immediately to the quantum qubit monitor, taking a Brain-eez on the way for his neurotoxins. His humble estate enclosed him like a prayer. Nothing, almost, was already more terrifying to him than television. However, he knew he must follow history.

His computer was aimed at the press corps. When Sir Arthur Eddington arrived in his tiny laboratory, President George W. Bush was gesticulating at a rare press conference, for a time making "word salad," but finally seemed to come out of his fit. He declared for the assembled microphones, "A dictatorship would be a heck of a lot easier, there's no question about it." An aide ended the conference, and the president George II grinned and waved as though in triumph as he exited.

Memphis, Tennessee appeared suddenly, as time was reversed by the collisions in the Large Array encompassing the solar system like a wedding band. It was a soulful city. A good man was shot in a moment of doom on the balcony of a cheap motel, never to see the Promised Land.

The Right Reverend Jesse Jackson, who would later run for president, was being interviewed: "A man must be willing to die for justice. Death is an inescapable reality, and men die daily, but good deeds last forever." This sentiment was Sir Arthur Eddington's fervent wish, as he was consumed by doubts.

Mahatma Mohandas Gandhi was strolling gingerly with his nieces through a throng of reporters, after giving the administration of India to a Muslim. A Hindu, like himself, bowed with hands together in salute. "Namaste," the man said, and arose, and revealed a pistol a shot. Blood spurted again.

"Ram," sighed Gandhi with his last breath, so that he might reincarnate well. Arthur sat down, petrified with uncertainty. As his cyclotron continued to accelerate, time was moving backwards increasingly. Anti-quarks were beginning to multiply towards the number of quarks, he knew. When would the temporal distortion end? he wondered, almost, uncustomarily, swearing aloud.

Mr. Brown in Highland garb was attending Her Majesty Queen Victoria before a select few interviewers. She sat with poise and equilibrium, which Arthur was almost envious of, except for his lack of ego. H. M. Queen Victoria calmly waved a fan. "We are not interested," she said, "in the possibilities of defeat. They do not exist." Time continued to speed up backwards, Sir Arthur Eddington noticed on his monitor. His television was leaping over the centuries. The Renaissance came and went, and Michelangelo's God ceased reaching for Adam.

The Dark Ages loomed. A single individual was interviewing a candid man of the cloth. "Do you believe sincerely in God?" was the question translated from Old English.

"God," was the return volley, "is not an article of faith. He is an article of clothing. I have seen poor men closer to God than thou..."

"Treason!" came the reply.

"The humble truth, for all to see," the priest declared.

Abruptly, Rome was sacked by the Visigoths and burned like a witch. The days of glory were returning. And at last time was slowing down. A crowd of the curious, if daring, authors pressed about the palace on the Palatine Hill. "Let them hate me, so long as they fear me," a drunken Caligula stated for all to hear, a horn of wine in one hand and a goblet of mead in the other. His laurel wreath was firmly placed on his short-cropped hair. Arthur stared at the anti-quark monitor intently as it appeared on his screen. He was about to cry out in dismay, but the counter began slowing down. He collapsed back into a comfortably adjusted desk chair, and breathed a temporary sigh of relief.

Caligulus took a deep draught of wine from his horn, and then some mead. The crowd was in fervid anticipation, for he rarely appeared. His toga fluttered lightly in a cool breeze. "I have existed," he pursued, "from the morning of the world and I shall exist until the last star falls from the night. Although I have taken the form of Gaius Caligula, I am all men as I am no man and therefore I am God!" Arthur could not help but gasp at this, and for a time his screen went dark. Arthur didn't know what was best, television or no television. But the anti-quark counter began to slow, at least. The monitor blinked once, twice, and the press corps were gone. The Palatine Hill was being rocked by a rare earthquake.

"Longinus," Caligula declared loudly, for the rest of the orgy to hear, "you're not having any fun. Enjoy yourself! What is your preference?"

Longinus: 'Everything and nothing, Caesar."

"That is not mysterious," Caligula replied coolly.

"Do you think this boy has been drinking?" queried a senile senator. "Bring him more wine!"

"If only all of Rome had just one neck..." mused Caligula, continuing to drink.

"Drink!" cried the other orgiasts.

"Caesar begged you," whispered the emperor coyly.

"I have no nerves," said Longinus.

"That is treason!" exclaimed the emperor, now quite drunk.

"Have him executed," commented the old senator.

"Give him enough rope..." Chaerea whispered to Longinus.

"And perhaps he'll hang us all," Longinus observed.

"My son must be born!" Caligula declared, nearly falling off his divan as he reached for grapes. But Julia Drusilla entered then, and informed him, "It's a girl."

"It is not a girl! Did you not hear Caesar say?" commanded the emperor. At that moment, in strolled the languorous Tullia Cicero, Cicero's daughter.

"Wine!" demanded the beauty, and everybody moved to serve, including the emperor. Then, Arthurs monitor went dark again for a time. The growth of the anti-quarks ceased abruptly.

"I shall order the army to attack," came a last vestige of sound, as Caligula the Mad was yet in possession of his wits. "Brittania is mine..."

"Jupiter shall spare the emperor," came Tullia Cicero's soft reply, as cunning as any vixen, as ferocious as a wolverine, as mad as Caligula.

"Tullia, my dear," emitted forth as sticky as syrup. Arthurs counter registered the rebirth of linear time. He was very nearly in a state of collapse, but his Brain-eez had improved his wits somewhat.

"The Sphynx itself is confused," Sir Arthur declaimed, and decided on Jamaican rum instead of his usual Bristol Cream sherry. "Three dead men on a dead man's chest!" he riddled. He sat, all alone, before the darkened monitor, and lit a pipe of perique soaked in rum. He felt ravenously hungry. He heard Caligula laughing, laughing with the scorn of the superior. Arthur nodded into an exhausted drowse, but would not fall asleep. Finally, he was swooning, and got up for his

Tesla coil to prepare an omelette. "Careful how you break the eggs," he admonished himself. Morning arrived on Pluto, barely more light than the Milky Way.

Nerva lay dying on his monitor. "Nerva, what's it like?" Caligula compelled. "Do you see her? Do you see Isis?"

"Warm, no pain...just drifting away..."

"Do you see her?"

"No."

"Lair! What is she like?'

"No."

"Lair!"

"The man who chooses the hour of his death is the closest to tricking fate..."

"Die, then!" Death was haunting Caligula.

"My dear, dear Tullia. Where is your father?" queried Caligula of Tullia Cicero.

"My father has died," came the cool reply.

"Caesar cannot be a fool!"

"No, he is dead."

"You are a swineherd. Pass me that amphora, moralist! And come to my arms!"

Arthur greedily consumed his omelette, then put a moistened cloth to his brow. He departed from the confines and up the space ladder, and turned off the Extra-Large Cyclotron Array which surrounded the solar system with the touch of a green button, reversed propulsion with a blue button, then descended back to his modest dome. He watered the plants, and remembered to switch on the negative ion and oxygen generators. His free energy machine glowed.

Anti-quarks were annihilating quarks, and symmetry was denied, but according to the calculations he made in his head, he was safe. He peered briefly out the asteroid-proof plate glass of his titanium dome at the distant earth as it eclipsed the sun somewhat. Earth was barely polluted, except for the people. Leper pits were being burned out with pitch. Swarms of insects were escaping the fires. Ever so slowly, time began to move forward again.

"My dear, dear Tullia, we have made plans," came Caligula's voice again. "We shall have a son." She knew silence was golden, yet silence gives consent...

"Have some more wine," she urged.

"Lucky girl," he said, "to lose your virginity to a direct descendant of the goddess!" Sir Arthur Eddington turned the qubit monitor off until later. Little did Caligula suspect that Tullia Cicero was slowly poisoning him. Nor did she know his will, which stated she be put to death if he died. But other hands than hers would decide his fate.

Caligula was blocked from entering his own marriage suite. "Password!" Chaerea proclaimed boldly.

"Scrotum," was the drunken reply.

"So be it!" cried Chaerea, and struck him down with his sword, to the envy of many.

Longinus entered the corridor. "Treason!" he declared. "And thank you!" But Chaerea had stuck a dagger into his own heart, rather than go to the Colisseum or the pits.

The guards came and hauled Longinus away. "You're for the ursus bear, for sure," one of them remarked.

Arthur turned the monitor on with a remote device. Bacon was frying with a sizzle and a pungency.

"Francis Bacon," Arthur jested to himself, although he regretted the swine. They always smile, even when eating.

But in the Colisseum were three giant boars, against one un-armored man with only a dagger. But Longinus was swift, and skilled. The starving boars were made swift work of, but Agrippa I, descendent of Herod, turned his thumb down, and a voracious black leopard and lion were released. This time, the battle was as quick as cats, and Longinus sustained many gashes. But he had struck at the eyes, and was victorious. Yet the thumb was turned down again, and the giant ursus bear was released, towering over Longinus with fangs and claws. He stabbed at the groin, however, but the bear leaned down in more hunger than pain. Longinus struggled in the bears grasp, his flesh being rent, and in a final gesture of defense struck at the slavering tongue, and slashed it out. The giant bear recoiled, and the dagger was driven into its throbbing heart. The thumb was turned up. The crowd roared by the thousands, and the gory Longinus was a free man. "Ave, Agrippa," he declared with a hail, and walked. Stylus's went to work on tablets for that mornings news. The press was only delinquent in noting who had really slain Caligula. As the news spread throughout the Empire and further, there was much rejoicing. But tyrants come and tyrants go.

Longinus was rapidly applying cold compresses, in evident agony, but with no less strength. His position in the legionnaires was still assured, and his pension of property in Gaul. He would live the rest of his days as a

Gallo-Roman in a modest villa with a maid-servant and a cook. Grapes for wine would grow in the gardens, and his cup would be filled into old-age. But his first night out from the Colisseum he had been treated to roast wild boar, and auroch with honey-drippings, and black bear stuffed with pudding. He was glad that in the Colisseum he had avoided being gored by an auroch bull. Fate, or chance, was with him, and the wine flowed freely.

Arthur had watched with fascination, as his screen again became dark, while his quantum computer continued to make its calculations. "Still symmetrical," Arthur mused. Time was moving forward again, and he finally napped on his Brain-eez.

After a few days it was the Dark ages again. The avuncular priest was put to death slowly with the burning of juniper and copper wire. Not even monasteries were havens. The Church persecuted itself.

The Renaissance came and went, rococo eventually became the fashion, then Romanticism.

Mr. Brown, in his Highland garb, attended H.M. Queen Victoria. She fanned herself, then ceased diplomatically for the press corps. "We are not interested in the possibilities of defeat. They do not exist." Mr. Brown accompanied her to her quarters.

Adolf Himmler was playing speed chess with himself. The United States and Britain had just rejected the surrender bid he had tendered, because it did not include Russia. He smoked as he played. His favorite word was "Jew," and his least favorite, "God." The barons were due soon for a brief conference.

Baron von Steifel commented upon Adolf Eichmann's progress with the death-camps, which would continue even after treaties were signed. The Baron von Gottingen entered, then von Salzburg, and, finally, von Liechtenstein. Whisky sours were distributed. Rommel and Goering made brief appearances to report, but were intimidated by the barons and swiftly departed. Hitler (Schicklgruber) was in retirement as Secretary-General. The Gestapo were relocating to Bangkok.

Joseph Ratsinger was at camp as a Hitler Youth. Already he was a budding linguist, later to become Cardinal Ratsinger and then Pope Benedict XVI. Sir Arthur Eddington watched his monitor with morbidity. But then he awoke as from a dream. At least the Pope could be trusted.

The Pope felt sleazy in his vestments. But he had to write. He changed his mind suddenly, and decided to flee in the popemobile. He swiftly grabbed his attache case, ignored his attendants on the way out, and fled.

"I'm headed for a better scene, man," he told his driver Albert, who was privy to his council. "Step on it! Take me to Andorra!"

Time was moving forward. General Waldheim was about to press the red button in the Pentagon and end the Cold War with Canada once and for all. But Sir Arthur Eddington was ready again, at the top of his space ladder. He reached up and pressed the green button. Time began moving backwards again, and more anti-quarks began annihilating quarks. Time sped up backwards, as only a cyclotron the size of the solar system could do. Arthur descended and peered into his qubit quantum monitor at the vision of Caligula.

"My dear, dear Tullia Cicero, what will Rome do without you?"

"You merely play at dice," came the bold and daring reply.

"You are merely a woman," Caligula said, feeling especially venal. "And your time will come. God does not play dice. And everyone has their reckoning. Live for posterity, my dear..." Time started moving forward again, but there were too many anti-quarks this time due to the cyclotron. Fundamental symmetry was becoming unglued.

Sir Arthur Eddington put down his journal. Man held the fate of the stars. Life would continue for awhile elsewhere in the universe. But Sisyphus could not push the stone up the hill, it rolled over him...the anti-quarks were spreading...only Caligula the Mad had his way.

CHAPTER TWO:
The Hex on Professor Hector

Professor Hector Alphonso, professor of ontology, was speeding along as he attempted to cross the Salt Flats back to the West Coast, after visiting relatives in the East. Nineteen seventy-five was a good year for metaphysics, but a challenging one for its professors. But he was almost ready for retirement.

In the gathering dusk, a lever descended in front of him for a train to pass. He stopped, and rubbed his eyes drowsily, then he looked up.

Hanging in the sky in front of him were three glowing lights, two smaller red ones on either side of a green light. Professor Hector Alphonso's car stopped running, but his mind was racing. He had never had an hallucination before.

The train passed. "I must have fallen asleep," he mused. But then he remembered the three floating lights, remembered them as clear as day. "There's something wrong with me," he couldn't help but think. But his journey back to Stanford University was uneventful, except for the nagging remembrance of the lights.

Professor Hector Alphonso was speeding across the Salt Flats on his way home, as dusk fell ever so silently. A train was approaching. He stepped on the gas and made his way passed the tracks. For some reason, his sense of relief was excessive, but he chalked it up to impatience.

But a few weeks later, his colleague at Stanford University, Professor Targ, began to notice something unusual.

"Did you know, Hector, your hair has turned totally white?"

"I had noticed that," Professor Alphonso replied. "But I don't think it's anything extraordinary. It can happen at my age."

"It seemed to happen overnight," remarked Professor Targ.

"Can we talk?" confided Hector. "There is something unusual going on. I've had the same lucid dream every night since I returned."

"Do go on," Professor Targ said with interest.

"It's like this: I'm shooting through space, almost approaching the speed of light, when suddenly the voice of God speaks to me and tells me to slow down because I'm committing suicide..."

"Fascinating," Professor Targ agreed.

Professor Hector Alphonso was speeding across the Salt Flats on his way home from the East Coast. A train was approaching in the gathering dusk, and he stepped on the gas to make the tracks. But he had committed an error in judgement, and collided terribly with the descending wooden lever, shattering it and his front lights, and bending his hood at a right angle. His head struck the windshield heavily, and he passed out. Strange lights were glowing in the sky.

He awoke in a hospital bed with electrodes attached to his skull. He grappled with his fate, and the electrodes, and ripped them off one by one, inciting a persistent beeping to ensue. But no nurse came. "Nurse?" he inquired blearily. But then his head hurt and he passed out.

Professor Hector Alphonso was speeding across the Salt Flats, racing to make time on his way home. In the dim light he almost laughed to himself about how man was always in a hurry. He sped past the "X" sign for railroad crossing just in the nick of time.

"Doctor," complained the professor, "I have not slept well in weeks. Is there anything you can give me?"

"We can always try Valium," replied the white-haired doctor mildly.

"I keep on having the same dream," Professor Alphonso continued. "It wakes me up every night."

"And what dream is that?" the doctor interrupted.

"I'm approaching infinity, and God is warning me to slow down, or I will die..."

"I see," replied the doctor, without a better answer.

Hector Alphonso was rushing across the Salt Flats at dusk. The train was approaching. He desperately wanted to make the crossing. But he was distracted by lights in front of him, a large green light with two smaller red lights on either side. He lost control of the steering wheel and swerved off the road into a ditch. His old Galaxy 500 Ford sedan smashed into a pile of rubble. This time he died.

But the body was never recovered.

Professor Targ was eventually informed, and wondered if his friend was wandering in the desert.

Dorothy Bensdorf of Salt Lake City read the news in the paper of a missing person. She stirred her pasta nervously. That night she was going to see the Mormon Tabernacle Choir at the cathedral.

"Only time will tell," she mused. She fed the cat, and went to don her finest apparel.

Professor Hector Alphonso was speeding along in his Galaxy 500 Ford sedan, trying to make it past the Salt Flats. Dusk was falling swiftly. The horn of the train broke the twilight air. "I can just make it," he thought. He sped up. He tore over the tracks in the nick of time. "I made it!" he said with relief. But something was giving him deja vu.

Hector Alphonso was speeding along I-80 to reach the West Coast. But a train was rapidly approaching. He stepped on the gas. But as he crossed the tracks his engine failed and he came to a halt. He just had time to look up and notice three lights in the sky, one green and two smaller red ones. Then the train ploughed into his vehicle like a sledgehammer.

Dorothy Bensdorf arrived back from the concert of the Mormon Tabernacle Choir with relief. She fed the cat again, and then looked at the headlines once more. But the newspaper was different: the missing person was not disappeared, but dead on the tracks. She threw the paper away.

Nineteen seventy-five was a good year for metaphysics, but a bad one for professors of ontology. Dr. Targ read the obituary:

"Salt Lake City, Utah. Noted Professor of Metaphysics Hector Alphonso of Stanford University was killed last night in an accidental train collision. It took the jaws of life five hours to remove the corpse, which was barely identifiable. The cause of the accident has been deemed poor judgement on the part of the driver."

Into the laboratory strolled Professor Hector Alphonso with a hot cup of coffee. "How are you, Russell?" he asked Professor Targ.

CHAPTER THREE:
April and the Lost Animals of Eden

Man once thought that beasts were to serve men. But after man's final Deluge, famine had struck the Beast called Man, while the animals were foraging, forever foraging. Some fed off each other, some fed off the land. Many years went by, since the legend of Eden, when they were named. Man was untamed, yet the animals, they said, were tamed.

This is my personal account, as one of the last of the dying human race. Before I die myself, I wish to record for the stars the stories of the animals who learned to speak to one another, who befriended one another, and who made enemies, like Man before them. I am still young, but I live now on few fruits. My country cabin has a wood fire burning. The animals come to join me in my loneliness, and I have listened to their stories. You see, my three parrots know their tongues, and I have listened deep into the night. And they have listened to me, as I teach them new words. We have a certain sympathy.

The night sky shone brilliant with no electric lights to dim it, as originally. Earth has come, ironically, full circle. Perhaps this is the meaning of time. I looked up at these stars, as they wheeled, with the fixed stars remaining to wish upon. Would such distant lamps hold any hope?

I named my three parrots "Mouse," "Bird," and "Norris." A few field mice had entered my remote cabin, and there was some mutual discussion being made inside. I then noticed a prowling mountain lion, and retreated indoors myself. The mice were starving, but the parrots well-fed. My pet cat, "Goat," did not notice the mice, he was sound asleep, and in any event did not eat mice, only fish. But he awoke with a start, hearing the mountain lion about in the nearby underbrush, as sometimes cats can hear quite well when asleep. His tawny fur bristled, and he proceeded suddenly to exit through the cat door. I had my reservations, and opened the top half of my door to investigate. But Goat and the mountain lion were making friends in the dawns early light, as not all animals do. A fire-ball of gas projected over-head, startling everybody, but they quickly relaxed again.

I took Bird the parrot on my shoulder eventually, and went outside to forage. Bird had an excellent sense of direction. Under the fading stars Bird took flight, and following as best as I could, over tumbled stones of my creek-bed and through a pool, we sank deeper and deeper into the forest. Miles went by, but at last Bird sounded the report, and it was excellent news beyond reckoning: a bee-hive had inhabited an old, burned-out oak. I used my flint to smoke out the bees. It was a shame I could not keep them.

The relish of the comb was enormous, and there was plenty. Bird perched on my shoulder and we ended this mission. That day I would have enough sugar energy to plant more on my sod roof and build statues of stone and mud and straw about, to my great amusement. The mountain lion had departed, but I figured it would circle around again. But a wolverine prowled later. This was certainly dangerous.

"Bear!" Bird cawed.

"Nay, wolf!" squawked Norris.

"It is a wolverine," spoke the more versed Mouse the parrot. He looked down at the hungry field mice, but wasn't interested until they squeaked. Then he would listen.

I determined that day to reserve a pet owl. The parrots required other company, and falcons were hard to come by. Later my fishing was successful, and the field mice and parrots and cat all well-fed.

That night I took Mouse the parrot for an owl-hunt. I logged many miles with Mouse on my shoulder.

"Owl?' I asked him.

"Bat!" he replied. We kept moving. Ultimately, we found a likely tree with a hole. I lured a screech owl with some fish, and quickly squeezed its legs with a noose. It flapped its wings, but then settled down for the fish. The owl I named "Athanasius."

Dawn was spreading again, like an eagles wings. When eventually the three of us reached my cabin by the stream, hungry crows were about, pecking at scattered seeds. A number of different "caws" could be heard. I went fishing again with worms and snails and maggot larvae as bait, and there was much regimen for all, even enough to hang a number of fish to smoke.

A young buck and doe passed by for food later, disturbing the crows only mildly. The buck and doe were evidently in love. Love, I mused, one cannot get enough of.

That very night came a loud scratching at the door. "Mouse?" I queried.

"Bear," Mouse replied, with his superior sense of smell.

I went post-haste to my cache, and withdrew my Walker automatic rifle. This was a matter that had to be dealt with. I opened the cat door and fired two shots into the brown bears hind legs. The bear was for the assembled animals that day, and for smoking, and for soup. This was tremendous good fortune. And when survival is at stake, man must be served by animals sometimes. A bear was dangerous in the neighborhood, too.

Athanasius the owl stared unblinkingly from where he was tied to his perch. The screech owl let out some screeches.

"Flesh, and marrow, and liver," I proclaimed out loud with triumph, and began that morning to sort through my wild herbs and dried mushrooms. I also decided to drain the bear, and make blood soup.

The next night I descried, just barely, a descending weather balloon. It passed as a shadow before Polaris. This was more good fortune. I decided to track it, so that I might make a tent of the balloon and a cupola of the basket. There with my flint-stone I could develop an excellent sauna, which I still had been working on.

Winter came chill to the Trinity Alps, but the sauna was complete, and very relaxing. Still, food became scarce. I set up taps on various trees for the sap, which I would boil in water, and had to travel far upstream for beaver-tail. The river was nearly frozen over, and the weir nearly impossible to detect, but I smoked them out eventually, and used and recovered some of my bullets. When I got home again I sharpened some of my knives on a stone, and kept the skin for any baby animals that might appear, as a comforter.

You see, I had fled long ago, as a youth, a dying civilization. I had murdered every man I had met along the way, for they wanted me for flesh, like the Donner Party, desperate. I had seen no women, and wondered if any had survived the feeding frenzy.

Winter turned to spring finally, and I dined on dandelion soup and baked psyllium bread. All seemed quiet, almost too quiet, as they say. The glow of the stars began to seem less beneficent, and I ceased my nocturnal ramblings, although I had been chronically insomniac for years.

"Polly want a cracker," Norris joked one evening. I could not remember ever teaching him the phrase. The parrots were getting smarter, and the crows, too. The crows began bringing scraps to my cabin, providentially, and in response to mutual friendship and considerations. With spring, my larder was expanding.

One night that rainy April, clouds broke at sunset, and I watched, lonely, Venus glow bright in the moonless sky.

Then a young woman walked out of the trees. She wore dark green woolen fatigues with a woolen shawl over her head. She was dripping wet. She approached, incautiously, hungrily. She had been losing weight.

"Your name," she panted, "what is your name?"

"Jeremy Balfour," I replied equanimously, although in deep trepidation and a burning suspense. The young woman was evidently very much relieved. I stroked my goatee and stared at her in alarm, not thinking anything, in fact trying not to think.

"My name is April," she revealed. "Do you have food?"

"Plenty," I responded, "of many kinds..."

"Food," she repeated.

I gestured with my arm, almost bowing. "Mind the cat, it's skittish with strangers."

"I won't let it loose..." April replied.

I stoked the fire, and offered the young woman a change of clothes. But I chose not to look, and be as discreet as possible. This blond slip of a girl was exceptionally gorgeous, I thought without any delusion of loneliness. She gladly accepted the change of clothes: her wool was soaked through, and she was shivering. "And now for food!" she almost gasped. Who knows how far and long she had walked?

I boiled some smoked fish in maple syrup, and also gave her a sizable chunk of psyllium bread to go with the fish, and a tin flagon of mint water to wash it down.

She did not speak, but consumed voraciously. The parrots, all three, watched with curiosity, although mildness. On the other hand, Goat the cat hid by the straw-bale mattress in a corner, with baleful eyes. April's eyes were light green, but with dark blue rings about, I could not help but notice. The effect seemed almost magical.

"I eat venison, too," she said with her mouth full.

"I do not kill deer," replied I, "unless necessary. That would be up to you..." I said hopefully, already wishing she would stay.

"I've been living mostly on mushrooms," she explained. "Food ran out months ago." But she did not look that malnourished, she had the glow of youth, and dilated skin. Still, I thought, she must be deficient. I gave up my last honeycomb to her for her dessert. She chewed greedily.

"Food is God to the hungry," I thought.

When she had finished chewing the wax, which would be made into a candle with a prepared flax stem, she collapsed on the bales of straw and fell asleep immediately into a Rapid Eye Movement state.

I tended the fire, and took some chamomile tea for sleep. The air was cold that night, but the spring thaw was in progress.

Another mountain lion prowled. I was out foraging, and there it was, as plain as day, foraging, too. This one was hungry.

Fortunately, I had remembered my Walker rifle, and still had a substantial supply of bullets, a necessity I had remembered those years before. If the forest made me miss once, I would have a second chance. I peered through the telescopic sights and fired, a direct hit to its abdomen. This was more food, and, I decided, a jacket to impress April with. I skinned it carefully, deposited the meat in my picnic basket, and strolled merrily home, giving up on foraging that day.

A red-tailed hawk circled high above. My heart reached out longingly. I knew April had to stay. But would there be other stragglers from the shipwreck of civilization? A cunning individual might stalk us at night. I kept my Walker handy.

April and the animals made fast friends. Goat the cat would purr and purr, uncustomarily, and Mouse, Bird, and Norris exchanged many chuckles. The screech owl Athanasius remained, thankfully, in respectful silence.

April was a creature of refined instinct, like the animals. The month of April came and went, and the rain-showers relented early, to our bliss. But one day April had a hunch, and chose to go to the ridge-top with my binoculars. An hour later she came rushing in, her eyes extra-dilated by adrenalin, and made this report: "Commando from bunker in Gortex and infra-red helmet headed our way!" A snake had entered my paradise. Both of us knew this one could not be trusted. I reached for my Walker swiftly, and April grabbed my wrist. "Be careful," she whispered, and kissed me on the cheek.

The commando had seen the smoke from my chimney. I could just spy him with my binoculars, rambling through the underbrush. He looked impressively strong, a survivor, ruthless. I assumed he might have bullet-proof Kevlar on by now, under his Gortex. He wore a Major-Generals helmet and an infra-red goggle on his left eye. I sensed he could detect my signature, and indeed he ducked behind a tree. I aimed my rifle, and waited. Several hours went by like this, with an interminable suspense. My telescopic lens had him dead to rights, though.

A pile of underbrush moved from behind the tree, and I spent all six bullets resoundingly. Birds with numerous calls took flight everywhere in the forest. I didn't care just then who heard, only that this barbarian was dead. I approached with utmost caution. He had been wearing Kevlar, but one of my shots had caught his jugular vein, blasting a hole in his neck. I disengaged him of all his supplies, so April would have his Gortex, which breathed, and I could hunt in the night with the infra-red goggle. There was also a Colt 45. pistol with a few rounds.

I hurried back to April at the cabin, which she was hiding discreetly behind. She had heard the six shots, but did not know their meaning.

"Bonjour, madam," I cried triumphantly, to her great relief. We went inside to calm down the animals, and then went back to bury the corpse. A crow showed me where to bury it. Only weeds would grow there.

The moon that night looked particularly full, and yellow. The flowers I had planted seemed to glow luminously. April joined me and we stared. Al-Hecka, the Bull's southern horn, set with a barest fringe of glow on some cloud.

But the days were bright now, and food plentiful. Yet Deneb was disturbing my dreams, which were fitful and restless, and I awoke in a cold sweat despite wool blankets. I would stay awake in the middle of the night drinking mint and lavender tea and writing this journal. I hope that someone worthy finds it, that they may avoid their doom.

One day in June Goat the cat alerted me with a hiss: in a corner of the cabin was a white scorpion. As swiftly as I could I threw my picnic basket over it. I then made a hole in the bottom of the wicker, and stabbed the scorpion, pinning it to the earthen floor.

Deneb haunted my dreams again that night, as April was awake showering in the sauna. I saw the fixed star become white like the scorpion.

I had intimations during the very next day that all was not right in the heavens, but I did not want to disturb April with the matter. Mouse the parrot, my second-closest confidante, said, "Let it be." So I could not tell April. But I took out a wooden shovel I had made, and I dug a wide moat, and I hauled marsh mud from the lake above, slowly and carefully, to fill it with. This took many days. I concealed the moat beneath piles of dry leaves and small debris.

Little did I know, the Starchild was furious, and the brethren of Deneb concretely ordinated to her service. Some things are better off not known.

But that summer, in the woods, a great thing happened: near a patch of briars and blackberries, now fruiting, I discovered an old patch of tobacco plants, no doubt left over from some antique miner. I carved a pipe out of Sycamore wood. April and I would enjoy a relaxing smoke.

Unfortunately, I had few books for April to read. Fortunately, I had the Complete Shakespeare, and she would be much absorbed by the stream, and by the fire at night. I tried to ignore her loveliness, her curly blonde hair and light green eyes with the blue rings, and her petite features. However, we smoked together in the sauna.

"Sky," Norris informed me one day. Animals, I knew full well, could be entirely instinctual. I kept my gun at the ready.

Deneb was setting, and I could not sleep. I sat in the rocking chair on the back porch, and waited, and listened. I heard a splash, and high-pitched squeaking voices. I rapidly circled the modest cabin and to my deepest ingrained horror observed monsters: their skin was grey, their eyes immense and entirely dark, their tremendous craniums bald. One of the three had fallen in my moat. With all my speed I spent six bullets, awaking all the diurnal creatures for miles. In the dark, without the infra-red goggles, I could barely descry the grey skin of the aliens. Sweating, I reloaded, and fired again, and then repeated a third, and again a fourth time. My fifth round depleted me of bullets. I donned the goggles and peered. But there was no signature of life, but three grey corpses bleeding. I was nearly frothing at the mouth. April ran outside and hugged me, and took me by the arm away from the scene and into the cabin.

"Relax," said Bird.

Norris rejoined: "If you can't take it easy, take it as easy as you can." I had taught him this years before.

"Grant us peace," commented Mouse the parrot.

I burned the three corpses on a bonfire the next day, after discovering in their grey suits lasers for slaughter and crystals for scrying and detection. The crystals I placed on the mantelpiece by some dried flowers as memorials, and the lasers I used to great advantage cutting wood, and made many artifacts and expanded the cabin for April. April told me of her insight: "It remains before the Fall."

"Forever," said I.

The cat and the screech owl were conducting a staring match. Field mice were congregating for warmth and scraps. I kissed April suddenly full on her rosy lips.

If this story reaches you, know that animals are your friends, and your lover may be coming over the hill, the one where the breeze blows the grass. "Amen," April said as I kissed her.

CHAPTER FOUR:
The Lost Book of Eden

I baked for April a pine-cone seed bread, and gave her sap in her mint tea. We then decided on a sauna. That summer I tamed a squirrel with bread. It made fast friends with Goat the cat and his yellow eyes. The birds all seemed in favor, too. I decided to name the squirrel "Pipkin."

But time was running out before winter. September was cold, and one night I went out foraging for many miles with the infra-red goggles and laser I had acquired. I had over-foraged the surrounding area, and the fish in the river. I found maggots and miners lettuce plentifully, but had to keep moving. The woods were running out, and I looked up to the high mountains and the lakes to fish. On the way I had set many rabbit traps. It was entirely against my nature, but April and I had to eat through the long winter.

In the middle of the night I reached a lake, and with my old twine and sharpened paper clip used maggots for bait. I didn't have to wait long for a sizable trout. This eased my worries, although April was a long way away and hungry. I made a fire with my flint and had just a little trout to keep going, saving the lions share for her. I also managed to catch several frogs. But this wouldn't help much with the long winter. I decided, with my laser, to be bold, and hunt bear. I clambered upstream from the lake to find a cave, and bait it with trout. Of a sudden, my infra-red goggle detected a signature. Before I could react, a starving bob-cat attacked. I dropped my laser, and felt blood drawn in great scratches (I had not worn the Kevlar, unfortunately, but was only in Gortex). I scrambled for the laser in a pile of lichen, found it, and attacked as well. The bob-cat was quickly overcome.

But I was in agony, and collapsed next to the bobcats corpse. My arms and chest were rent. I would have remained immobile from pain, but I went into seizures thinking of April. I was bleeding heavily. I knew the smell of blood might attract other dangerous animals like mountain lions and bears.

After an interminable wait of draining blood I somehow found the power, thinking of April, to try and stop the bleeding. I put dust into my many wounds. But I doubted severely that I could make it back to April soon in my weakened condition. I decided to skin the bobcat and eat some raw, first the eyeballs and then the rest of the brain.

Then instinct got the better of me. I did not need another wild animal attack. I had to flee, no matter how weakened. I threw the rest of the bobcat into my satchel, and steadily tried to retrace my steps as fast as possible down from the mountains.

But the woods were where a bear might hunt, for maggots and honey mainly, and I was in a numbing agony. I kept the laser at the ready, and one of my old knives from when I fled the city, sharpened steel from a river rock.

I could hear a bear ahead. I slowed down. I was nearly in a state of collapse, yet at least the dawn was breaking. The bear was starving, and faster than I anticipated. It charged with a great crackling of undergrowth directly towards me. I could let it get close, so I set the laser, and paused until I made eye contact, and then hurled the laser directly at the bears head. It sliced through flesh and bone, and I had won. But I collapsed with exhaustion and pain, and passed out.

I was awakened hours later by a crowd of turkey vultures picking at my wounds. I waited only momentarily for regained strength, and slashed one with my knife. The others only fluttered. I laughed miserably at their presumption, and crawled on my hands and knees with my knife. I got one more, and the others flapped over to the dead bear. I managed to take a draught from my flagon, and eat some maggots and miners lettuce. The sun rose over the eastern mountains and began to warm me. But I had lost much blood. At least the nocturnals would probably be in hiding. I passed out again.

I was again awakened. I was crawling with ants. But these small creatures turned out to be providential, and serendipitous. I heard more rustling in the underbrush, and crawled to my laser. A cougar appeared and snarled with a fierce hunger, drawn by the scent of my blood, and with lust in its eyes. I kneeled, with laser in hand, and awaited the leap. It was forthcoming, and I slashed at extended legs. I got one, and the cougar was incapacitated. I sliced off its head to be certain.

I knew I must certainly gather myself, and, thinking again of April, wiped off the tickling ants. I used my laser on fallen logs, found ivy vines for rope, and produced a sled. I had to clear a path, again with my laser, but its battery finally ran out. I collapsed again from the agony and exhaustion. But I remained awake, as I knew I must. Slowly, ever so slowly, I pulled the cougar and two turkey vultures to the sled, and with my knife dismembered the bear so that I could haul it to the sled. I struggled over rocks and debris as best I could towards our humble cabin, barely making progress with my heavy sled-load. I crept along, doing my best to move and still ignore the pain of my many wounds.

At last, I heard a whistle off in the distance. It was April. "April!" I cried. "Coo-ee! Over here!"

April found me. "Oh, my God!" she exclaimed, and took my stained hand. "You poor dear! How bad is it?'

"As long as I avoid infection, I'll make it!" I swore.

"Can you move?" she asked, desperate.

"Yes. Help me pull this sled."

We made it back to the cabin. The first thing I did was make compresses of shredded Gortex, as April put the larder to smoke. Then I took an extra-hot sauna, to sweat out the fever, and wash out the dust from my significant wounds. Then I lay inert in the sun on a warm rock by the river, after drinking a deep draught.

April was busily baking bear stuffed with boiled pine-nuts, sap, and mint leaf, and roasting the maggots which she would wrap in miners lettuce. But I would be laid up for weeks with my wounds. For the time being, however, we had enough food. And April would check the rabbit traps. I drew her a map of their locations, although barely able to move. And pine-cones were plentiful. Pipkin the squirrel was enjoying a nibble of them.

Later that September, as I was healing, a wretched fox terrier came to our door, another straggler from civilization. We gave to the poor dog smoked cougar to eat, and adopted it as "Maurice." It was well-trained and would eventually help us with the hunt.

But I became obsessed again by visitors from a further land, the now-foreign stars. Could it be that we were sitting ducks? We had no bullets and no laser, and we could either flee into the mountains or head back to the dangerous cities. I hoped and I prayed, though not a religious man. April consoled me from our volume of Shakespeare: "'I never knew so young a body with so old a head,'" she read from The Merchant of Venice. Then she lay me under wool, with a warm fire under the mantel.

On October tenth I decided to rouse myself. I invented from skin and twine a sling-shot. I would not kill the crows that assembled for snacks, but would make other birds my mission.

April was busy planting miners lettuce. I joined her for awhile, then went searching for pine cones. I even gathered pine needles for tea. But then I felt tired, and sat down, leaning against a large log. I fell asleep. When I awoke, night had fallen, and I knew immediately April would be worrying.

But when I looked up, I was confronted by another alien vision. But this one was entirely different from the three I had seen before. It was a hulking ogre, with a drooling snout, and in steel armor, along with a helmet with great horns on it. I would have thought I was still asleep and dreaming, only the odor was intense.

The ogre spoke into a mouth-piece and adjusted an ear-piece. "How are ya?" came the translation in English.

"Not too well," I decided to admit. "I poisoned," I then said, just in case it was hungry.

"Been looking for a hermit," the creature said, "am seeking wisdom...from your doomed race..."

I paused, but his features did not register impatience. "I do not know your needs," I stammered hopefully, "but I have an excellent book at home..."

"Give me your best, if you can spare it." It could not smile, but its eyes lighted up.

I did not regret my Complete Shakespeare. The alien seemed reasonable by sound. But I was incapacitated and completely overcome with weariness. "Can you carry me home?"

"Will do," he replied with a trace of humility.

When we reached the river, I told him to remain. I took a deep draught, noticed a fish caught in a pool, and barely proceeded to the cabin.

Upon entering, April began to recite, from King Henry the IV, part two: "Rumour is a pipe blown by surmises, jealousies, conjectures, and of so easy and plain a stop that the blunt monster with uncounted heads, the still-discordant wavering multitude, can play upon it."

"Here's your book," I told the troll.

"Thank you," his translator snorted, and he made his way, shambling, back to the woods.

That winter I placed around the cabin many target stones. After a month, I was expert with my home-made slingshot. I often would go to the forest, and kill everything I could, as April checked the rabbit snares. We passed our leisure time carving poetry into large river stones. April had a special touch:

"I live by humble means,
In my humble house,
Where parrots speak of my humble dreams,
And listen to the squeaking of a mouse.
But of all the schemes, love shines aloft,
And I fly forward, without wings,
To find his arms, and oft.
The dog lies down with the cat,
As smoke from our tobacco, soft,
Rises to the heavens, wherever they are at,
And I listen, as I sit,
For my lover, he doth know of it:
The tongues of animals he knows,
And has survived,
Through the stings of his morbid, deathly throes,
And come back to me and thrived.
Ever will I love, and call,
My sweetheart from the woodland hall,
My sweetheart from the woodland hall,
As love rests on high, is All,
And the stars at night are seen to fall,
And if he dreams not lightly, I wake him, withal.
The stars that shine with happenstance,
Send glowing down their light, in trance,
And if I read aright, they do not speak of chance,
But destiny, the heart that yearns to be carefree,

And so I give sweet charity.
I call him by his name, 'Jeremy...'"

CHAPTER FIVE:
Beauty Fierce as Stars

I am in the dark night of my soul, as I sit here, alone, in the hollow vacuum of space. But it was my wish, and for twenty years I scrimped and saved to escape the pollution and over-crowding of Saturn, with its artificial atmosphere finally decaying into waste. The sun is a dim light as I orbit the uninhabited Planet X. I expected nothing less than the darkness of my soul in such utter solitude. I am far, far away from the civilized and uncivilized lessons of men, with only insomnia my most certain companion, except for the bounty of my hologramic food and my sleep aids, which do not seem to work in space, and then there are the small artificial environments I generate to guide me in my solitude. Today I sit by the waves with a pina colada. Yet existential angst has gotten the better of me again.

Still, it was my wish, to escape the company of men and search through darkness for the ideal life of a hermit, whose satisfactions must be in self-reliance. It is the supreme test of darkness versus light, to find oneself in utter solitude, dependent on no one, except, perhaps, the least agreeable of creatures: oneself. But I abjure to coddle myself, or allow such luxury as I have to make me passive. I wish only for release.

The disease of insomnia is slowly, progressively eating at my mind and brain. Sometimes I seek a greater vacuum still, the ultimate rest. But this folly, presenting itself daily, I ignore, for I have come to find my place, not the peace of the final resting place, but the rest few men of our age may achieve, inner peace of mind, of heart, of soul.

I gave up my pina colada and sank into the waves of my holodeck cubicle, and let the artificial, salty waters cleanse me, however temporarily. I then dressed in my finest three-piece, put tobacco in my pipe, and sank into a stuffed chair before my television. My antennae detected the news from Earth, which went from bad to worse, as food riots continued to spread, while on the moon a few lucky stragglers ice-skated amidst the confetti of New Year's Eve, 3014 A.D. The rich got richer as the poor got poorer, as President James Garfield had predicted long ago, twenty days before he was assassinated:

"Whoever controls the volume of money in our country is absolute master of all industry and commerce, and when you realize that the entire system is very easily controlled, one way or another, by a few very powerful men at the top, you will not have to be told how periods of inflation and depression originate."

I took some more of my inefficient sleeping pills, doubting their success. I had not slept in seven days, and, as is well known, insomnia is progressive. In any event, I desired no sleep: unconsciousness to me resembled death, and my dreams were restless, and better off avoided. The television with all its ghostly light depicted horror after horror, until I was too restless to continue and inserted my favorite comedy disc for any diversion it might provide. The starkness of the contrast only disturbed me more, so I went to my telescope, if only for another view into the hopelessness of the Abyss. A comet was making its way, once again, to pass by our star system. Its heated trail through space wilted away into nothingness behind it. As I had done: I had left no trace of my exit from civilization in my one-man craft. This was necessary, as you will see,

At last, after six months adrift, I brought out my dictation pad: "My name is Mark Knight. For twenty years I labored in Saturn's classified and secret underground bunkers as a physicist, working feverishly on the neutron missiles, as Saturn prepared for the predictable onslaught from Earth. I never knew who I worked for, only that we were called the Green Day Project, or GDP. The last year of my many labors included de-coding the decontamination unit and alarm system. As a thief in the night, I penetrated the appropriate locker, and absconded with the appropriate uniform for dismissal. With my credit card in pocket, I managed my unlikely escape to the surface, and with the greatest alacrity I have assembled this ship, and penetrated Saturn's security grid posing as a lunar mining drone.

"For my disappearance I am a wanted man, as perhaps a double-agent working for Earth. As I idle here by Planet X, I can only wonder if anyone might locate my existence. Either I live untouched up in the heavens, or I go to hell. Or, perhaps, there is a purgatory."

I set the holodeck cubicle for ten after midnight by a peaceful lagoon, and watched the rising of a fabricated full moon. It reminded me of long ago, as a child savant on Earth. My love was for literature, yet early practicality would rear its ugly head, and I worked for a means of escape, driven onwards by desperation and followed closely by a sense of futility.

In my beach chair I was almost falling asleep, but alarms rang from my antennae and telescopes. I was being approached. All my senses and instincts came immediately to bear: a labor camp was no place to end up.

But I was a sitting duck. I hailed the approaching craft in English, and hailed the heavens with an "ave Maria."

"Are you alone?" came the response, distorted and muffled for concealment.

"My ship I call 'Rover' and my robotic dog I call 'Apollo,'" I radioed back hopefully.

There was a long pause. Perhaps the other party suspected I had space sickness.

"My craft has been demobilized by Berkeley. Only emergency propulsion has brought me this far. Prepare to be boarded."

"What must be, must be," I thought. I did not bother arming myself, but went back to my midnight lagoon with a gin and tonic to wait.

There proceeded various creaks and clangs from my docking port. A figure entirely concealed in suit and helmet then entered my holodeck sanctuary. I half expected a "retriever" android. The mysterious figure, its suit emblazoned with the stars and stripes, removed its helmet to reveal a ravishing young woman with curly blonde hair, deep blue eyes, and full pink lips. "I'm sentient," she declared immediately. But certitude in such a statement was lost on me. "Where is the food?" came her next melody.

"Out and to the right," I chose to calmly reply, and sipped my gin and tonic. The fabricated moon was setting, and the unreal stars of the holodeck began to shine brighter. My solitude was now shattered.

The apparition of the young lady soon returned, hungrily devouring a stack of pancakes with maple syrup on top. "I barely made it," she explained. "Security precautions at NASA have leveled preemptive strikes at the rest of the solar system. I stole the most armed ship I could. I must have killed hundreds of satellite denizens on my way here." I expected as much, be she human or android. She extended a gloved hand. "Ayelet Xavier Womersley, existence classified," she pronounced triumphantly, her eyes shifting mysteriously from deep blue to grey. I tried to remain passive, and reveal nothing with my own hazel eyes, and shook her glove politely.

"Mark Walker Knight," I responded without emotion, with the control of a physicist.

She removed the glove and rolled up her sleeve, revealing a cybernetic forearm. "Do you have batteries?" said the figure named Ayelet, shaking out her blonde curly hair. "I lost it in the Swiss Conflict," she explained of her arm.

"Out and to your left," I stated in return.

In a few brief moments she came back, and dipped her arm in the hologramic water of the lagoon. "Ahh...it was beginning to itch," she said. I observed that her eyes were turning back from grey to blue.

"Martini?" I suggested, half expecting it to be my final words, at this point.

But she said, "Yes, please," and evidently was going to allow me to live for now.

"Shaken or stirred?" I replied.

"Once I have the martini I'll be stirred but not shaken," Ayelet jested. I though it absurd that I had been contemplating my own weapons, and made her a martini on the rocks without further adieu. If she was a "retriever" android, perhaps she had investigative programming which caused the delay. The martini was gone at a gulp. "Fill 'er up!" she said. I obliged. She was not being importunate. "How much energy do you have?" came the ravishing young beauty's next question. I was then thinking to myself that Earth would never defeat Saturn.

"Terra-watts. Enough," I stated hopefully.

"Ahh," she replied, and then suddenly, narcoleptically, drifted into a deep sleep, ignoring the last of her pancakes. I left the lagoon to watch TV.

Earth was eclipsed by Planet X, but I still received reception from my distant former home. At first there was only a tone, and then: "This is an alert of the Emergency Broadcasting System." I knew Earth's magnetic shields and interception missiles were no match for Saturn. In any event, Earth's elite intended to destroy the rest of their population. My sensors could just detect the neutron radiation flares as missiles penetrated Earth's atmosphere. I was a devout pacifist, but my survivalist instinct desired no survivors. My ethical constitution was torn. I receded to my private antechamber to organize my weaponry. I was still in doubt of my visitor, who had shattered my sleepless nerves into increased insomnia. But I had an inkling from the shifting colors of her eyes of what she required, so I manifested a supply of heroin hydrochloride tablets. But I pocketed a taser just in case there was trouble. I then returned to my television to watch the last, peaceful inhabitants of the moon be destroyed by missiles from both sides. Anarchy was finally consuming the human race, on New Year's Day. My television went black and silent, and I was left to ponder the starry skies from my window. I hoped that Ayelet Xavier Womersley, whomever or whatever she was, had not been followed. But I began to relax, knowing that such resources were limited to the very few. My superior at the Green Day Project was one, I knew, but he would be consigned to a bunker for the duration. It would not last long, however, as a relentless fury consumed planets, moons, and asteroids into the Qliphoth, the lifeless shells. Then there was only radio silence.

"Ayelet" did not awaken that day, nor the next, as the artificial sun of the holodeck cubicle came and went. But I was consumed by my increasing insomnia, and the lingering paranoia of a possibly unknown danger. A NASA operative with a cybernetic arm was not a nemesis I desired to confront. I injected her as she slept with a large dosage of heroin hydrochloride, and then went back to observing Planet X. At last, I discovered what I had been looking for: a cave for concealment in. I guided my modest rocket and Ayelet's docked ship impeccably into position in the dark, except for the slight glow of phosphorus, which gave off a ghostly effect as I contemplated my doom. I could not take her life, she might be innocent. On the other hand, she was probably a hardened commando, and, perhaps, not even a real being, but an android. Yet when she awoke, refreshed and sated, she had the luminous glow of a real person. Her eyes, however, were transformed back to grey.

I decided to give her the benefit of the doubt. As much as I desired the cave of a hermit, perhaps human contact was not unacceptable. And she was beautiful, ravishingly so. I tried to ignore this, but found I could not. Her blonde hair framed a perfect face, the eyes large and full of life, only equalled by the fullness of her lips. Except she possessed an equally desirable figure, as I could not help but notice as she stripped down from her space-suit to her military skivvies to bathe in the lagoon: she was petite at the waist, but with a buxom wealth of the bosom, full round breasts greater than melons which her wet clothing clung to like my eyes. I offered her more pancakes, and she again ate ravenously. She seemed to be pretending not to notice my stare.

I put an orange into her hand. She looked at me and pouted as though I were a sneaking rascal. How many men had she denied? I thought. Then I remembered myself: there may be a snake in my Eden, I must proceed slowly, and learn, if I could. She merely snickered under her breath, a traitor or a friend.

Her cybernetic forearm flexed about the orange, and she tore it open voraciously. I imagined that she would do this to me. Was she my adversary, or could it be some game? My mind settled comfortably into the latter, even as I had lingering doubts. The truth of beauty, however, was horrifying, for it intimated death. Perhaps she wanted what was mine, or perhaps she would share: she had said she was sentient, but that was somehow no less terrifying. She humored me over the trifle, and said, "There is no rhyme for 'orange.'"

"How about 'lozenge?'" I tried.

Ayelet giggled ever so slightly, but I did not detect a trace of warmth. Yet my conclusion had to be she was not a "retriever" android. Still and all, a NASA commando was potentially equally dangerous. There were a number of fates I could imagine. Intensively screened and trained, strong of will, and unyielding, there was no telling how many people she had killed. I felt like I lived at her luxury. But nevertheless, I was overcome with her beauty, the tremendous fullness of her bosom on such a slight figure. But her giggle seemed to say, "Wretched idiot."

Later, at night, I attempted my best ruse, to find out more as soon as I could. "Shall we go for a swim?" I determined to say. She looked at me with penetrating eyes, now light blue. She was progressing between the dark blue and the grey. Her eyes seemed to say, "No man is my equal."

However, she partially conceded, and said, "Perhaps that is a good idea." My robotic dog "Apollo" let out several mechanical barks from the next room.

I lead Ayelet from our midnight snack back to the holodeck cubicle and the lagoon, where the artificial sun was setting with a bright orange. Ayelet Xavier Womersley began unbuttoning her skivvies without pretense, until she hung, revealed enormously of breast, with equal nipples. I could wait no longer with the suspense, but unzipped her pants. They fell to the hot sand. I pushed her to her knees, and she bent over willingly with her rear exposed to the humid air. "Please," she groaned, and she had not known sex in years. I grabbed her hips and sank within. "Oh, God, you're big," she moaned. The petite curves of her buttocks were tight around me. I forced myself deeper. "Oh, please," she groaned again, and I thrust hard. She began gasping. We climaxed mutually with the setting of a brilliant sun.

I ordered pink champagne to accompany the after-glow. The event did not answer the ultimate equation, life or death, but I took great satisfaction in her yielding, and finally slept.

When I awoke, Ayelet was not in sight. Drowsily I searched her out, and found her in my antechamber with my collection of books and weapons. I noticed she had replicated a platinum ring to wear, which was a positive sign, unless, of course, it was another ruse. She proceeded presently to recite to me a snatch of William Butler Yeats:

"'I made my song a coat
Covered with embroideries
Out of old mythologies
From heel to throat;
But the fools caught it,
Wore it in the world's eye
As though they'd wrought it.
Song, let them take it,
For there's more enterprise
In walking naked.'"

We agreed with a look not to wear clothes. Nagging doubts would yet plague me, however, for what if she was merely buying time, all the while coveting what was mine, and leading me, as if I was senile, to my ultimate end? As is so often true, what is lacked is clear knowledge.

Back in the control room, Saturn was broadcasting victory, without casualties, while the other side in the war, the asteroids, moons, and planets, were utterly annihilated, with casualties of thirty billion plus. The prime minister declared, "We do not believe in torture, we believe in relieving torture. For all intents and purposes, we have saved mankind from a far worse fate of disintegration and decay into famine, massacres, and riots, and perpetual pollution."

A member of the Saturnian press corps stood up and boldly asked, "Is it possible there are spies among us?"

The prime minister put it simply: "If so, they are now without directives."

Commander Garrett Stryker had strolled boldly down a neon corridor in the small township of New Hope, Saturn, until he had located a convenient saloon. There he brooded over the finest vodka he had purchased with his stolen credits. He had been Commando Ayelet Xavier Womersley's shadow, but had lost her in an asteroid melee. With the end of the war, all his NASA directives had been superseded, but Commander Stryker was nevertheless fueled by an insatiable desire to discover Ayelet's whereabouts, if she was still alive. His mission, he knew, was to access secret telecommunications involving any survivors of the war. He also knew that any survivors must be far away from Saturn, probably concealed in the hidden recesses of the Outer Planets, all of which were annihilated by neutron bombs except for Planet X. And spacecraft were classified and hard to come by: they were either the province of the government, whoever they really were, or the shadowy black market, likewise disguised. Instead of attempting to ingratiate himself on an unknown government, he chose to pursue the black market. The necessary items would be expensive, although could be limited to minor food provisions, oxygen sufficient for a few months, and some propulsion. The difficult part would be getting Saturn's superior magnetic shielding to yield. For this, he must achieve security clearance, for nothing less could penetrate the barriers, no amount of propulsion would avail. Blackmail, he thought, by way of kidnapping. Yet he was already in danger of becoming conspicuous. But his desire for Ayelet would drive him on. His will was replete with icy determination, a superhumanhood that was the pinnacle of the age. He left the dimly-lit tavern, and ducked down a side street. The next passerby would lose his life over his identification bracelet. Then, at least, Commander Stryker would be mistaken for a citizen. And he collected more credit. The body he dismembered to cover his trail, and slipped the pieces down a sewer grate.

The rumor of the black market lead him onwards to the industrial hub of New Pittsburgh, by rail. As inconspicuously as he could, he prevailed upon more victims, accumulating more credits for his mission.

Ayelet and I were busy skinny-dipping at a beach under a yellow moon. The titanium of her forearm gleamed. After a luxurious soak, we returned to shore and she oiled the mechanical parts. She did not appear self-conscious about her deformity, incurred during the

Swiss Conflict. There was much of her past she would not reveal to me, although she was my omnipresent temptress. I decided not to pry, but was confronted still by nagging doubts. To be a NASA commando meant screening for all personality defects, yet those with successful determinations would still possess hidden conflicts in their psyche. For one, the inculcated survival instinct, which I knew so well, was at war with common human decency. For the time being, however, she seemed content to let me live. We left our beach and watched a disc of light comedy, completely naked. My one regret was I could not carry my taser. As time went by, a preemptive maneuver began to weigh on my conscience. But taking a life was abhorrent to me.

Ayelet had not offered to show me inside her own rig, which remained docked with mine in our cave. Months went by with only pleasant, if deceiving, events. I was lulled, as they say, into a false sense of security.

Commander Garrett Stryker had developed his machine, after many months of hard labor, as Ayelet and I relaxed. His space-craft was now completely jerry-rigged. He strode boldly into a consulate one day and spent all his remaining credits negotiating a code from the appropriate official, who saw nothing wrong with allowing someone to escape. It was only people seeking entrance through Saturn's security grid that he was concerned with. Not to mention he was in fear of his life.

The artificial atmosphere of Saturn passed away below Commander Stryker, and he signaled his purchased code by radio to the Green Day Project headquarters: "MB1222parrot," classified investigative transport. For the brief appropriate moments an opening formed in the magnetic grids, and he maneuvered his way through, headed for Planet X. He suspected, however, that he would be followed as a precautionary measure.

Robert "Bob" Randolph was at the helm of Green Day Transport 555. He had been greedily awaiting himself an opportunity for some action.

Luckily, I had purchased the finest antennae the black market had to offer, a black market which had existed for centuries of clans, often bribing complete investigative teams into submission. It was an era of ultimate corruption even among the races survivors. It was for some hint of this corruption that I searched Ayelet's eyes, in the color of her transforming iris's as they shifted from dark blue to light grey, especially when she indulged in heroin hydrochloride.

The alarm tones wailed: spacecraft approaching. With a gesture of her cybernetic forearm, Ayelet superseded me at the controls. She disengaged her craft from mine, and with the touch of a few buttons, a code unbenownst to me, ejected her craft speedily in the direction of the first of the two incoming ships. With supra-charged magnets her craft engaged that of the first intruder, and with another press of a button on my console, the nuclear pile of her engine flared noiselessly in space. Commander Garrett Stryker of NASA was no more, except drifting splotches of frozen blood floating in the vacuum of space.

Major Robert "Bob" Randolph laughed with glee. Ayelet and I intercepted his transmission back to the Green Day Project headquarters: "Mark Walker Knight discovered. Will proceed with caution to take him alive for indoctrination back into Green Day. Major Randolph out."

Ayelet pinned me to the lead floor. Titanium claws had distended on either side of her cybernetic arm about my neck. "You did this to me!" she screamed, a hoarse yet hollow sound which echoed into the other chambers of our enclosure. "I'm not leaving until I get everything I want!" She kissed me roughly full on the mouth, then her ruby lips trailed down my neck, which she bit voraciously, sucking blood. I was paralyzed in simultaneous ecstasy and horror as her lips trailed down to my girth, and she sucked hard for a full half hour until I finally reached orgasm. She wiped her mouth, and retracted her claws. She then got up, bare naked, and raced to my antechamber, gathering up a laser rifle, even as Major "Bob" Randolph was proceeding to dock. But he, too, was prepared with a laser, as an inbred superhuman. There in the decontamination unit, with a few brief flashes, the nearly equal duel was decided: the major had lost his head, and Ayelet had lost her other forearm. I had watched cautiously on the video monitor.

I raced into the unit with a compress I had hurriedly manifested, as Ayelet kneeled in evident agony. I tied the compress off tightly at the elbow. "I can help," I assured her. "I'm a physicist," I finally admitted.

"It was Saturn, then," Ayelet gasped. We both knew there would be more pursuers soon. I tore back to the main controls and navigated our ship from its cave, shrugged off the gravity well of Planet X, and ignited all the main thrusters on "high." The Rover shot out into the inter-stellar void.

Back at Green Day headquarters Major Randolph's life signature had registered null. All about the Green Day projects pentagon silos slid open, and twelve dozen missiles shot upwards with superior anti-matter propulsion.

I was racing back to the control center, and, as swiftly as I could manage, gathered the replicator pad, and, as a brief afterthought, Apollo the robotic dog. I shoved them through a portal to my hidden escape pod, and consumed with wild trepidation, yet no less haste, went back and gathered the naked, bleeding Ayelet into my arms, and carried her to the escape module. It was cloaked with a reverse doppler effect produced by crystals, where our only hope lay. In all caution I used only mechanical thrusters so as to leave no signature, and we floated away from The Rover in "The Tyger." My first thought was then for Ayelet, as she lay awake from pain. I gave her a powerful injection of heroin hydrochloride, and she passed out.

I looked through the view-scope at the receding Rover. Availing myself of terra-watts of energy, I pulled all emergency shielding levers to induce a supra-powerful piezo-electric field. Twelve dozen missiles collided with The Rover behind us, and we were thrust by the anti-matter explosions, without gyroscopic equilibrium, spinning head over heels further away from the distant sun. Artificial gravity failed us for some time in the raging tumult as we were catapulted by the explosions, and we were bounced roughly about from walls to ceiling and, finally, to the floor again. Green Day presumed victory, but we had narrowly survived.

I took no care of my many bruises and scrapes, but went presently to work with the replicator controls, to manifest solid-light holograms of titanium and electrical wiring. I continued to inject Ayelet with the heroin hydrochloride for an intervening week while I worked steadily upon her arm. When she was properly anaesthetized and the work was done, I let her come to.

"Where are we?" she asked immediately, even through her stupor, as training had taught her.

"Headed in the direction of Fomalhaut," I replied unhelpfully.

The first thing she remembered was the loss of her other arm, but then she remembered me. "You are a physicist, for sure," she said, flexing both her arms. She hugged me with the tightest of grips, and I winced from my unhealed bruises and wounds. "I think I can trust you now," she capitulated. I attached the replicator to the ceiling and we both took a shower. After this, she asked me in jest, "Do you have a lozenge?"

"An orange lozenge," I returned.

Apollo the Dog said: "Rough."

CHAPTER SIX:
The Celestial Meadows

It was the winter of our discontent...

The largest military confrontation in history was finally over. Of the seventy million deaths of World War II, thirty million had occurred on the Eastern Front, from combat, starvation, exposure, disease, and massacres. Many of these were civilians. Yet Ivan had survived, and straggled back to Moscow pale and emaciated. He was still indebted to military service.

But Tatyana Ilyushin Zharkov was at last able to immigrate. She kissed Ivan's haggard cheek, which ran with tears, as the train for Switzerland pulled into the station. For all the perils that Ivan had survived, this was the crushing blow from which he would not recover.

"You really mean to?" his thin voice whispered, as though still doubting.

"I must," Tatyana replied, weeping equally.

Tatyana Ilyushin Zharkov peered through frosted windows at the wrecked tanks and frozen bodies half-buried in the snow. Her diamond necklace was like the frost, but her enclosed heart would not harden, yet nor would it forget. She would look back, and the past would ever seem more real than the day. The chatter of the club car came to her as though unreal. The inexpressible magnitude of tragedy weighed upon her, and from a distance she would never be truly separated from Ivan. The taste of quinine lingered in her mouth, bitter-sweet, like memories of love from long ago, when she and Ivan had known peace together.

As she gazed out the frosty window, her soul was transported up to the stars, which shown like so many snowflakes. All the saints were gathered there in her mind, and they called out, "Do not despair!" But it was too late, unless an unlikely destiny should intervene. Or likely, for what is destiny is the soul's contrivance, and what could be more likely than the soul, she thought. But as the tears would not pass, the long years would, in her modest home beneath the Matterhorn in Switzerland.

She would sit out in the cold night by the river and watch the stars, some fixed, some wheeling overhead. Alcor, "the Neglected One," was faintly visible, and reminded her, over the years, of Ivan, the love she had left behind. Akrab, "the Scorpion," reminded her of her own mortality. She was maturing into the life of a mystic, not religious as she had been as a child, but believing in profundity. The stars seemed to hold all the answers. Bellatrix in Orion called to her, a tale of heroes vanquished. But most of all it was Navi, in Cassiopeia, "Ivan" backwards, that reminded her of her present, solitary life.

Tatyana's beauty would not leave her, as she matured so did her comeliness. Yet she remained alone, preferring to respect the past, and only make the stars her future. Polaris, the lodestar, was unshakeable, and Tatyana, despite her grief, would remain true and faithful. Spica shown bright, the constellation Libra was ever balanced.

Yet if there was one thing as constant as the stars, it was the wars of men. The last years of the 1940's would pass, with civil war in India, in Greece, in China, and the 1950's were ushered in by the Korean Conflict. Sometimes, like fate, the stars, like the ways of men, shown baleful. For fourteen years the Vietnam War raged, as if there were no end in sight. And Tatyana wondered into maturity whether mankind was forever fated. Almost one and a half million people died in Vietnam, again many civilians, and this was followed in turn by a still greater tragedy, the Cambodian Holocaust. As Tatyana watched the stars, ever so slowly she aged, and yet did men, women, and children fall. Iran and Iraq lost one million souls to nothingness. The war between them was ended decidedly in the desert trenches, as Iraq doused both sides with chemicals. Man was finding new ways to kill, and new ways to die. The light of the sun was blotted out once more by the moon, and Tatyana was left to wonder where in the sky her souls destiny lay. The wars seemed uncountable, like the stars, but in her loneliness the days would be counted, her fate driven forward through the unfathomable, insurmountable shrouds. Finally, the year was 1990, and wars were raging as Tatyana reached her 77th year. She sat by the river below her Matterhorn, and saw a series of falling stars. The one thing more inevitable than war, she mused, was her own passing.

Yet the years would turn in her favor, and at last, gracefully, she reached her 100th year. It was the year 2013, and a new world. Some wars were ending, some new wars about to begin. She drank a gin and tonic in celebration, despite a sense of melancholia. The taste of quinine lingered in her mouth. Tien Kwan, "the Celestial Gate," arose quietly in the east, and Tatyana Ilyushin Zharkov had her foreboding.

The very next year, on her birthday, she passed away in her sleep. She had dreamt of Zanrak, the "First Star of the Celestial Meadows." She had left her body, departed her humble villa, floated away towards Zanrak far above. The stars had parted for her, like saints, as though in greeting, even as her life slipped before her eyes, back through the decades of wars and calamities, through the meadows of the countless dead, through to Zanrak, the first star of the celestial meadows. And there, there, weeping unconsolably was Ivan, weeping for his lost comrades, weeping for the children of war, and weeping for the years, for his lost love, Tatyana. He had passed away long before, still pale and emaciated.

In her dream, he looked up, eyes blurred with tears, and said, "O my beautiful, my lost goddess, I see you here, now, beyond the grave. All that once was, has passed away. But after we have gone, the weeping stays." She did not wake up.

CHAPTER SEVEN:
The "Tycho" Necessity

Chistina La Vey, Commander of "The Richtofen," turned off automatic propulsion and reversed thrusters. She was within six feet of the moon, wide awake on amphetamines for the landing. It was almost entirely dark outside, and colder than the abyss. Next to the landed Richtofen were crates of supplies deposited by a balloon from an unmanned orbiter. Nearby, she knew, were the caves of ice she was to investigate. She took a last puff of nicotine through a vaporizer, which left no smoke in her environment, and proceeded to don her suit and helmet over her unusual features: she was petite for an astronaut, slim yet with ample bosom, and with a head of red curls down past her lithe shoulders. But all this would matter not.

She was not only an astronaut, she was also an archeologist, and been of wits with forensic deduction. She did not expect great mysteries to unfold necessarily, but who could say what might be found in the lunar caves?

Next she donned her backpack, replete with rappling gear for lowering herself into the cave, and a number of ham sandwiches and some Tang to drink. The hatch bolted open, and Christina was exposed to the lighter gravity as she stepped with weighted boots onto the lunar surface. She felt an almost orgasmic thrill of weightlessness as her first step carried her thirty feet, and she danced towards her destination of the nearby mountains.

Sophocles "Tycho" Maskeleris was recruited by NATO (the North Atlantic Treaty Organization) for his far superior Intelligence Quotient, 220 by some estimates but outside of test perameters by others. He was not a creature of convention, but experimentation: he presumed nothing. At age thirty-two, perhaps a trifle old for an astronaut these days, his hoard of knowledge was greater than most achieve in their lifetimes. He spoke eleven languages, including the otherwise extinct Old Norweghian, played fluent violin and piano, and was one of the highest ranking chess grandmasters on Earth. Although slim of build and not high on the scale of physical prowess generally, his extreme determination had set a number of Himalayan records, including his mastery of Annapurna 2, an especially dangerous mountain to attempt. He was also adept at counting cards. But it was his ability to deduce from the ordinary, and from others expressions, that made him especially valuable to his mission.

Sophocles "Tycho" Maskeleris performed a more perfect pass-by than Christina La Vey had. But in the mountains of Mare Nubium it would be a rough landing. He ended up seated at an angle. He jovially sucked on a packet of rum before debarkation.

The year was 2020, and although Sophocles considered many things strange, stranger was his old desire, inherited from his grandparents, for the Greek spirit to emasculate the German Republic finally coming true. Or not so strange, he thought with a touch of vanity, even hubris, that he himself could not deny. He was prepared for every lunar eventuality, and his space gear was armed to the teeth. But, as he usually surmised, craft was more powerful than violence. And the Germans did not suspect, according to all gathered intelligence, at least.

Christina was also not a creature of convention. She came open to experience, seeking adventure and loving life fiercely. Sophocles was more of a reserved type, and typically preferred books to humans, perhaps a flaw of the hyper-intelligent.

By the time he was exiting his craft, Christina La Vey was rappling down the steep walls of a nearby cavern. "Tycho" could just make out with his telescopic lens her pulley nailed to the entranceway. He rambled forward, leaping over rocks in his thick rubber soles, whistling Schubert.

Christina hit an overhang. She peered down the chamber, lit by the light of her helmet. At the bottom of a drop of perhaps a hundred feet the cavern began to level again. She began rappling downwards through the grey rock.

Had Sophocles been a mean man, he could easily have cut the rope right then, and the potential future strife would be over. But he was not mean, he had merely inherited generational bigotry, or more exactly national pride and a passionate love of freedom. And of some people he was curious. Whereas the German Republic did not expect that he had been recruited as an NATO astronaut, he knew full well his parallel. There had been, as usual with major space missions, many classified meetings to discuss international implications:

"Classified: Top Secret, operative Christina Szandor La Vey, Intelligence Quotient: unknown. Memory capacity: unknown. Physical qualifications: unknown. Notes: natives psychism tested three times by the National Security Council of the United States, in "secret." Native is obvious, daring, ambitious, playful yet ocassionally hostile, has issues over single foster parentage. Plays ping-pong expertly. Ultra-refined character judgement. Enjoys humor of a sexual nature. High psychism quotient." But all this would become naught.

Sophocles looked over the ledge, and almost said, "You - who?" despite the soundlessness of the void of space and the helmets. He briefly considered his microphone, but declined his own offer. He wished to meet her face-to-face if possible. He initiated his own rappling progress, and descended into the night.

The cavern split off into different directions. Sophocles followed Christina's rope. "Perhaps we will find Davy Jones's Locker," he mused happily. Technically, however, according to mission control he was under orders to terminate the German agent. Sophocles emerged from a hole in the ceiling of the greatest cavern. There lay the object of the test: among stalagtites and stalagmites were deep patches of ice, colder than colder, crystal-flashing in the light of Christina's electric helmet. Sophocles himself had turned off his.

Christina was drilling away with a laser, making a deep incision, more than she could possibly carry back.

Sophocles watched the scene for some odd hour as she dug deeper and deeper into the ice of mystery. He peered through his thick lenses and telescope, and could just espy Christina carefully removing a hair and an insect of some sort, and played them delicately into petri dishes. As the ice yielded to the laser, she found the greatest mystery so far: there, laying profoundly for what must have been centuries, was a giant humanoid skeleton, no less than twelve feet tall, Sophocles judged from his distance. It was all bones, so the ice must have come later. In its hands it gripped a box made of wood but sealed with silicon. Christina would not dare risk the contents to the atmosphere, and so deposited the box into a satchel. She then removed the heavy skull of the skeleton with precise laser sheering, and decided this was all she could investigate for the time being. She could sense that something was wrong.

Sophocles "Tycho" Maskeleris sensed this, too: she was on to him psychically. He avoided her sight and sped in his superior mountain-climbing fashion up his rappling line. He knew he was way ahead of her, as he reached the top. He briefly considered again undoing her rapple and letting her perish with her finds, and indeed this was incorporate with his mission directives, but he would not proceed. Self-indulgence intervened, despite the potential danger. What he did proceed to do was enter Christina's craft and make himself comfortable vaporizing tobacco and sucking on rum packs.

But Christina did not join him. She pitched a tent outside her craft, he could just espy, and outside the tent began carving a small sample from the giant humanoid skull, for radio-carbon dating. The skeletons box lay unopened beside her.

"I've been had!" Sophocles protested jokingly to himself. He was feeling rather rummy now. He never enjoyed being suspected of anything beyond the good joke or gimmick. He wished it might be love, but knew it was probably war. He placed a small quantity of TNT below the girls chair, with a three-hour fuse, and then continued to inspect.

Christinas dial was plain to see: the skull was about 200,000 years old. "That is not so old," Sophocles mused.

But just then, an immense triangular craft replete with yellow lights sped over them at tremendous speed, and then was gone.

"That's not any side!" exclaimed Sophocles, as Christina was rapidly taking down her tent and gathering her belongings. Descending back into the cave now seemed like a fool's errand, to say the least, but a mission was a mission, to some. Sophocles had his choice: to abandon his own mission, or follow the trail of darkness and descent. Christina had packed her belongings, but was busy with her morphine drip, or was feinting, or both. Sophocles slipped out of the docking bay of her craft and sidled behind a rock.

"You!" came the cry over his helmet microphone. "Who are you?"

"Metaphysically speaking? I'm not sure. After all, what is the nature of the soul, and is there free will?"

"Bite your tongue, mortal! Who do you work for, and what is your name?"

"My name is Tycho, and I work only for myself. If I have free will, that is."

"How did you follow me this far without my noticing?" the psychic queried vehemently.

"Some of us are innocent," Sophocles replied.

"That's a good answer," Christina admitted, thinking of that German baron she had stabbed one night. But she had had to do it. Christina was swiftly looting her space craft, and she rolled all her belongings in the tent, which she attached to a rapple. "Come down here if you dare!" she said.

"You will need my supplies, ration as you will. We will say nothing of daring." But she disappeared over the edge.

Sophocles waited until his TNT had detonated, then relocated his own craft away from the crevass of night, up the nearest mountain to the highest point he could land on, nearly at the top. He would have hours of warning before she made it there, if she could figure out the direction. But it had been a feint. She had climbed the cavern up again, and, in the lighter gravity, heaved her haul upon her back, strapped it with vel-cro, and bounded across the Mare Nubium plains for a secret German base beneath one of the countless craters.

Sophocles had not noticed her leaving. The feint had been successful. And he was waiting like a sitting duck for that Unidentified Flying Object.

After a drunken day of solitaire, he decided to descend. Mystery was worse than death.

Sophocles merrily glided down the rappling ropes, but into pitch darkness. He emerged briefly in the ceiling of the ice cave but did not spy her there. But other caves lead off in other directions. His choice was retreat, the better part of wisdom. When he emerged, he did not detect her tracks in the dust, because her shoes had "blowers" attached. The Germans had won, for now. But what had they gotten away with?

"What else can you tell us?" Baron von Trapp proceeded.

"'Tycho' is deity," Christina nearly sighed.

"You know the rules: no fraternization. Especially with the enemy."

"Everybody is my enemy," Christina complained.

"The pay is good," von Trapp reminded her. "Now what do you think of this skull?"

"I think it's the result of cloning," said Christina, still hot-tempered.

"Why, for workers?" von Trapp continued.

"Probably for a wild goose chase. And to scare away the recipients."

"Ah, for what? What is it they're hiding?"

"Isn't it obvious? They're hiding the space race. If it is revealed they live in fear of the progress of others, their own position might be compromised."

"Ah. Cigarette?"

"Cigarette, please," Sophocles asked mildly.

"Oh, all right," the construction worker replied. There was something irresistible about Sophocles in his top hat and coat-tails.

Market Street in San Francisco was bustling with activity, with foreigners, with brokers, with the plague. Sophocles had spent his latest stipend. He lit the cigarette with a match, and somehow the odor of sulphur seemed to suit the environment, he laughed to himself.

His next mission was temporarily thwarted: he was waiting for Christina to come down from the moon.

She arrived shortly, and was whisked away by limousine to the German Secret State Police headquarters beneath San Francisco, to their remote viewing laboratory.

"What do you see?" Baron von Trapp, secretary-general, asked at first.

'He is standing on Market Street, smoking a cigarette."

"What is he?"

"He defies description. Even his name defies description. But he is a relative of Pavlos, King of Greece, but does not consider himself a part of the royal family."

"We will send in our operatives immediately. We'll get our answers," von Trapp assured.

"I have doubts," Christina said.

Sophocles "Tycho" Maskeleris had boarded the "N" Judah line going uptown to a NATO bunker for debriefing and to receive his next stipend.

"You and I are worlds apart," he nearly sang.

"He can hear us," Christina intoned in the lab.

"Who does he work for?'

"Nobody."

"Everyone works for someone or some thing."

"He wants world freedom."

"Where is he now?"

"Underground."

The NATO inspector peered at Sophocles intently yet mildly. Sophocles was cleaning his thick spectacles with a cotton kerchief, monogrammed with the crest of the

Greek royal family. "Do we go back to the moon, that blue cheese?" queried the inspector for Sophocles's benefit.

"I have a nemesis, and she is more psychic than I. She wants to marry me or kill me, I cannot tell which. Perhaps it is both."

"You'll be paid overtime for the duration. Please be careful, very careful indeed. Here is your stipend and maps of the daily routine."

Tycho was much relieved. But he had to state, "There may be more in the caves of ice. I have a hankering to return. I made eyeball contact with an Unidentified Flying Object. The area is of some interest, although entirely unsafe."

"We will cnsider it your next mission. Be wary, and please don't deviate from our shadow teams. We'll try and protect you. By the way, who does this nemesis work for?"

"The German National Police. She's in league with the barons." This depressed and worried the inspector to no end.

"Which is safer for you, here or the moon?"

"I cannot tell. The more the variables, the less liklihood of deduction."

"Quite so. May we be established."

The interview was over, and Sophocles departed the heavily gaurded bunker to the outside world. His first destination was the Mandarin Hotel at Fisherman's Wharf, positively swimming with NATO agents. Room 222 depressed him as a number, but the room service and complimentary bar was excellent. He kicked off his heels and put up his feet, and proceeded with a pipe.

A day went by where he did nothing but rest and relaxation. Then he began creating his list of the prospective german barons and baronesses, the collective leaders of the Fourth Reich. According to his psychism, they were organized around the Baroness von Goldwasser, the Ipsissimus, the supreme leader, of the group. His list he mailed off the next day. He then ordered an armored limousine, and, following his maps, picked up smokes downtown and then headed to Clement Street for sushi. All went well, until his way back, when stopped at a street-light his limo went under assault by semi-automatics. The driver waved dismissively. The car could handle lasers. But two of the wheels were deflated, and they limped back to the Mandarin, obviously being followed. Men in grey trenchcoats lurked within the corridors, searching out his room number, but were soon put to death by Chinese acrobats. The place was a mess, but no matter, the hotel was owned by NATO, who proceeded with a clean-up effort.

After seven days the mission was ready. Sophocles taxied uphill to the Mark Hopkins Hotel, which had been made a hollow silo inside. His rocket sat within, and he boarded on the fourth floor. The roof of the hotel was unhinged, and with water being separated from hydrogen, and replete with sound muffling devices, the rocket sped into the atmosphere. The eyewitnesses would never be credited, of course, because the media had an agreement with the government not ot print anything detrimental to national security.

Deep within German National Police headquarters Christina La Vey boarded her own craft. The Gestapo had not been fooled. But this time, Sophocles would make it to the moon first.

He drove in a steel-glass bubble upon a ship about the size of a killer whale, of black steel. Utilizing all propulsion devices he steered directly down the cave, so that he could not be detected on the surface. All his radar-jamming devices were also active.

A large manhole opened on Market Street, and Christina ripped upwards in her geodesic lunar lander. The time moved quickly, and she bounced to a landing near the cave. Mare Nubium spread out before her.

Sophocles was wasting no time and was busy cutting through ice with a laser. He quickly came to a computer notepad of antiquity, and, utilizing his linguistic capacities (he knew eleven languages, including Old Norweghian), he swiftly interpreted the hieroglyphs on the cover: "Aboriginal Quantities of the Continent," it read. He placed it carefully in his duffle bag and dug further. He discovered his true destination, a quartz crystal ball. He then quickly replaced himself in his machine, and glided down one of the intervening passageways, deeper into the heart of the moon.

Christina rappled in a few minutes later, and presently noticed the extra work on the ice. But there was no victim present. She would have to report to the Baroness von Goldwasser directly. She spent the next several hours digging apart the ice and found a few more electronic books, a mummified cat, and an ancient astrolabe, but no further skeletons. She departed in frustration. This evidence proved nothing extraordinary. But there was plenty of more ice to explore among the stalagtites and stalagmites.

Sophocles no longer detected her heat signature, and removed himself from his place of hiding. He then, purposefully, set out to follow Christina's trail. All intelligence had stated the Fourth Reich had not developed faster propulsion systems. His mission was to prevent her debriefing.

Sophocles caught up to Christina's ship in the stratosphere of Earth among tremendous monsoon thunderheads. He fired several photon torpedoes at the geodesic dome as it descended, but they richocheted. Then all was wrapped in the gloom of the clouds.

Christina saw her escape, and shot towards research headquarters in Gottingen, Germany. But she left a trail through the clouds which Sophocles followed straightly.

Sophocles attached himself and his cargo to a glider parachute, and ejected, with his craft aimed by auto-pilot to heat-seek the fleeing Christina. A fiery gas ball flared briefly over Berlin, the result of the collision.

Baroness Jennifer von Goldwasser sat steady in her parlor audience chamber, drinking a gin and tonic and admiring the ornate antique tapestries of the Crusades. "Guinevere," came the butler, "a guest to see you."

The Baron von Trapp saluted. "Heil Himmler," he ejaculated. "Himmler" meant "heavens."

"Ache tung," the baroness replied.

"Agent number one has been terminated, according to our chip. The lunar mission is delayed. Other programs are advancing on schedule. Congress is easy to bribe, and our challenger canditate is soon to become president, by all the polls."

The Baroness von Goldwasser was dismayed over the lunar failure. "Next time," she replied pointedly, "I shall go myself!"

Christina Szandor La Vey was no more but atoms. Sophocles "Tycho" Maskeleris did a little Grecian jig in his Ritz-Carlton suite. He decided to use his three days on earth wisely, and concealed as though reading a newspaper, strolled to the headquarters building.

"A complete animal compendium of Pangea," the chief liguist informed him of the book he had found. Sophocles pocketed an ipad copy of the translated hieroglyphs. On his way out, he pocketed a light machine: this might prove useful eventually.

Jennifer von Goldwasser was glad to leave her apartments in Berlin. Her petite frame leaned over the railing of the luxury liner, and her extended nose twitched. She would not risk a plane flight, despite the urgency, until once she had made it to San Francisco, which remained the only known location to fly out of safely.

Sophocles had his plan, and landed out in the plain of Mare Nubium. He placed quarantine beacons all around his football-shaped craft, to attract attention. He then set up outside an electric light show and placed at the center the crystal ball he had unearthed on a pedastal. He sucked on a rum packet reflectively.

He strapped below his chin his conicle helmet with the drilling bit on the top, and donned an exo-skeleton of titanium and a jet pack. It wasn't long before a triangular craft hovered above. Sophocles shot up to it and collided neatly, boring a hole into the exterior. He was onboard at that.

But humanoid aliens surrounded him rapidly with lasers and other hand-held devices, wearing differently colored costumes.

"Take me to your leader," he tried in the language he had learned from the book.

One of the meaner-looking aliens cleared his throat and aimed his weapon. "I am the leader," he said.

"I don't suppose you're open to diplomacy?" Sophocles interjected. He shot a dart with a small plutonium pile through the ceiling of the corridor, and pressed the timer in his pocket to five seconds. "Bon voyage, gentlemen," he entertained, and, reversing gravity, descended with great rapidity to the lunar surface again.

First the light in the ship glowed brightly, then a flare emitted from its flank, then its lost its hovering position and plummetted down into the mountains.

A luxury cruiser appeared a few minutes later. Jennifer peered out the window at the quarantine indications and the light show surounding the crystal ball. "Something isn't right here," she said to the captain. She donned her suit and helmet and rubber boots, and pressed the eject button. She floated down to the lunar surface not far from where Sophocles lay hid. She attached a device to the door handle of his ship that decoded it, and entered unknowingly.

"Here, here!" came a cry from the interior. "A Goldwasser! A vodka with gold flakes!"

Jennifer was off-guard for the first time in her life. She removed her helmet and breathed the air, and applied a wrist-rocket to her hand, a favorite technique. She entered the chamber, but all was empty, except for the drink on a bar and a bar stool. Then, the craft detonated.

Sophocles "Tycho" Maskeleris would await his recovery vessel patiently, counting cards. After several days NATO arrived, and there were profuse congratulations from a dozen men and women who had been watching on close-circuit television. The Fourth Reich would clearly be weakened temporarily. Now it was their trustee, the Baron von Trapp, that Sophocles was after.

But Baron von Trapp sat comfortably isolated in the lead bunker below Market Street, smoking an Havana and sipping sherry. A photograph of Eva Braun, Hitler's secretary, was perched behind an ornate antique desk. He decided to write more in invisible ink, this time to Baron von Gottingen, in the margins of the San Francisco Chronicle, to be delivered later. A restructering must occur, with himself as the new temporal head. The giant cloned skull stood on his desk, a friendly reminder of the supremacy of death.

The Hilton was replete with NATO runners. Their courier system was busy bringing supplies to room 222 for their exemplars usage. Sophocles sipped pink champagne, relaxing more than usual, even. But his psychism was galvanized towards its maximum.

He combed his hair, beard, and mustache and replaced his monocle, and donned his top hat and coat-tails. He pressed the pager button for his driver, and a few minutes later climbed in the back of his limousine. "Market and Hyde," he said to his old friend.

A stately blonde in lapels and skirt was about to make a deposit in a postal box. Sophocles blew a poisoned dart out the window into her neck, and she collapsed. He retrieved from her the latest San Francisco Chronicle, and in the limo painted it with iodine. The invisible scrawlings were made legible. He brought these himself to NATO headquarters, after making xerox copies for himself. A number of murders occured along the way.

He could tell it was the writings of one man. But it was not signed, except by the crooked cross, and was written by the left hand. Sophocles chose to dine out that evening, and attached a silencer to a Walker automatic.

The first course at the Hilton was delicious, the second only better. By the time he had finished dessert, he was quite full. A gentleman with a neatly-trimmed mustache and wearing a grey suit and tie approached his table.

"We meet at last," came the offer, clearly a showdown to the death.

Sophocles was not distracted, but admitted, "You know me but I do not know you. You have me at a distinct disadvantage." He knew this conversation would be brief, and readied his Walker under the table.

"My name is not my most important fact," came the steel-cold response, as Baron von Trapp contemplated the Luger pistol in its holster just behind a lapel.

"There is no truth," Sophocles tried. This indeed created momentary delay, as the baron was unusually disgusted.

"Your name is...von Trapp," Sophocles deduced with the necessary time. He fired through the tinted glass table and watched the body fall backwards with satisfaction. Sophocles removed the baron of all of his papers, his pen, his pocket-watch, and lastly his kerchief, then strolled casually amidst the uproar to the elevator, motioned others to stand aside and let him alone, and took the looted plunder to his room. Now he was having the time of his life, as he knew only a few remained, and he had valuable items. The pen, pocket-watch, and kerchief were all monogrammed. The paper didn't seem to have any use except for stock quotations.

Sophocles switched on the television, which blared of the latest riots in the Middle-East. He concentrated with all his equanimous delight, and plasma surged in his brain. He thought to himself: "So the letter was for...Lady Gottingen!" He was successful, he knew. "And she is...Eva Eichmann, Hitler's great-grand-daughter! The imperatrix!" He left the television on and water running in the tub, and hailed his limousine. "To the airport! Not San Francisco, Oakland, it's safer!"

The Germen bullet-train glided along at 200mph as it hovered over its ceramic rails. He admired the mermaid statue out in the harbor, and debarked jovially at Central Station. The Sheraton Hotel was replete with luxuries, but he hurried to room 333 for self-diagnosis. He held up his looking-glass before his pocket mirror and did a quick iridilogical exam. His eyes were dilated sufficiently. "She stays in this very hotel," he intuited, "but in an unlisted number. Why, that is,simple: it must be by the maids closet at the back. But no one can enter due to the electric shock field." He sat down for television in German, which he knew fluently, and smoked his finest in his pipe.

Baroness von Gottingen, unmarried daughter of Maxmillian Eichmann, sat absorbed fully in the latest missives. None were positive. But she had secondary and tertiary plans. Her cultus would continue.

Sophocles ordered room service, for lasagne and Gatorade, and offered the porter a handsome bribe for his costume, which, after some importunity in negotiation, was accepted.

He then placed a special tap on the phone, and listened into the night to a jumble of competing messages. Finally, a melodious voice, dripping with honey, ordered room service. He got dressed in his new-found costume, and took the San Francisco Chronicle with him.

The maid-servants closet was in the basement. He got off there. The door next to it, he noticed by tapping, was sound-proof.

He had his enemy cornered. He pressed the bell, and momentarily a slot opened in the door. "Room service!" Sophocles declared. "San Francisco Chronicle." But the door did not open.

"Hand it through," came the langourous reply. Sophocles produced from his pocket his electric prod, and turned it up to full power. He slipped the newspaper partially through the slot. When he saw a bejewelled hand appear, he prodded it with significant pressure, and the electric field of the room was initiated. He was immune, as his grip on the prodder was rubber and would not conduct. From within came a horrible moan combined with crackling, and then the smell of smoke, like burnt hair and flesh, and some Egyptian rayon.

"I thought the Fourth Reich were aliens," Sophocles said out loud to no one. "Illegal aliens."

With little difficulty, as the Baron von Trapp had remained secluded, Sophocles "Tycho" Maskeleris was able to assume his identity with the barons monogrammed affects. He knew there would be more - the Baron von Gottingen would get wind of the deceasement.

Sophocles was on his way by bullet-train to Athens. He entered the club car confidently, in top hat and tails and his finest monocle. The seat opposite the individual was vacant. "May I?" he pried

"At your leisure, I am sure," came the Baron von Gottingen's reply. The rest of the car was packed, with agents of all sorts taking pictures. Sophocles noted the red signet ring with a single red eagle, and also the sly look of malevolence above a sleight trimmed mustache.

"He's greedy," Sophocles thought as privately as he could. He produced brand "555" cigarettes, and made him his offer. "Cigarette?" he proferred. The baron had his own supply, yet it was somehow rude to decline this gentleman. Sophocles sat, and unfolded the Baron von Trapp's kerchief as a bib, much to von Gottingen's amaze.

The baron extracted his own monogrammed lighter. He had had psychic, plasma-filled intimations of the meeting, that was why he was there. He figured a brief pause, at most. He lit the cigarette. Gunpowder sizzled, then exploded, blinding the Baron von Gottingen on the spot. Sophocles tucked the kerchief away, left the Baron von Trapp's pocket-watch, and stole away conspicuously into the next compartment, then the next.

A seat was available next to a little old Jewish lady, her snow-white hair in a kerchief. "Is this seat taken?" Sophocles inquired lightly.

"No, indeed," came a smiling reply.

"Pen?" Sophocles proceeded, producing the Baron von Trapp's gold and ebony stylus. "It will help you with your thoughts. Or you can pawn it."

"Why thank you, my dear," she gladly accepted.

"My pleasure. Totally," Sophocles "Tycho" Maskeleris proclaimed.

"Next stop, Athens!" the conductor cried out.

CHAPTER EIGHT:
The Domino Effect

It has been many years now that I have worked for the Black Ops of Central Intelligence, "the Company," ironically in competition with a NASA secret intelligence unit, which wanted the aliens alive.

Amongst sprawling towers and shining advertising screens lay Old New York City, "the Big Apple," lit with light and lurid with sin. My electro-magnetic imaging device detected another boarding a taxi going uptown on Fifth Avenue: a man with two hearts. This one was exceptionally overweight and yet impeccably dressed in tuxedo and bow tie. My own shabby trenchcoat and ancient tailor-made suit made me fit in to the suffling masses, unlike my target.

I turned into an antique alleyway between two churches. I had sureptitiously placed a magnet under the bumper of the taxi. Eventually, Sarah and Rodney would swing by with their unmarked white van, still a typical "Company" vehicle. I smoked impatiently by the dumpster, making review of the passerbies: a middle-aged woman with a baby stroller, looking suspicious, a man with grey sideburns and a grey suit with that days New York Times folded under his arm, and finally two Jesuits in brown robes who entered one of the two small churches on either side of me. I stepped on my cigarette in frustration. Finally, the white van pulled into the alley, and Sarah called out, "Get in, Terrence!" I clambered through the rear door into the vault of detection devices. Rodney took off his headset.

"Hello, Mister Sheffield. Where to?"

"I'm guessing the library." I handed him the magnetic imaging tablet. "This one's more overweight than the rest. But the library is too suspect. We'll wait for him to reach a restaurant. Despite his sense of style, I suspect he likes junk food: we'll make it look like a heart attack. Have our shadow ready to haul him away in one of the fake ambulances, before anybody else arrives."

"As you say," Rodney replied.

But I was too sure of myself. In reality he was going to the restaurant first. We were missing a valuable clue. His taxi stopped before a gold-filigreed McDonald's. The three of us parked and followed him in, where he was consuming three Big Mac's, an evident delicacy. I fingered the button in my pocket with its electromagnetic pulse aimed at his hearts. But then a slender man in a black suit and thin tie sat down between my pulse and the obese alien. I was compelled to hesitate.

I listened with the boom microphone embedded in my ear. The slender, dark-haired, clean-shaven man was speaking hurriedly to the unshaven, obese extraterrestrial. "They're aiming. Stay by my side and we'll hop in a taxi. We'll see if we can lose them." But the man had his doubts, given all the shadow teams in the shining, sprawling city. So the pair pursued plan B. They entered a taxi, then exited opposite, ducking low, to enter another taxi. They directed the driver to the Waldorf-Astoria Hotel nearby. They knew that Central Intelligence's resources were spread thin, whereas NASA's were not so much. "Agent Calhoun," the man said, 'shaking the fat aliens hand. "You're welcome to Maryland. But I wouldn't leave here until you change your appearance, or have heart surgery."

The man gifted the NASA agent with a token silver coin, then proceeded with wads of forged money to rent a suite, the very suite where the scientist Nicola Tesla had lived. No sense in not going in style, he reasoned. But by the next day he would look like an unkept hobo pushing a shopping cart of piled garbage and belongings, drinking a beer in public.

Terrence Sheffield was searching uptown. "Damn!" he swore. "Now ain't that a bitch! That NASA operative had us all the way!"

'You'd think at least there would be private phone calls," Sarah complained.

Rodney on his headphones was listening to funk music. He took them off. "Falling short with the Prime Directive, again?" he snickered.

"We can't allow time-travellers, or alien intelligences," Sheffield swore. But NASA's directive was the opposite: we come in friendship, as they say. The CIA was a foreign branch of government. "Time-travel especially," Terrence added.

That very moment in a lead bunker somewhere in Maryland they were talking about that very thing. "What we have here," a NASA director was explaining, "is a situation too entrenched and therefore too out of control. Any suggestions, gentleman?"

A lovely young alien with freckles and curly red hair responded, her twin hearts beating. "Our travel in space and time is one-way. It is one thing to get somewhere, quite another to get back."

"Precisely," said the NASA director. "What's done is done, and no amount of temporal interference can alter the results we see in the present. For all we know, we have already altered the past in the future."

"Damn!" swore the red-haired girl. "I shouldn't have got in that time-travel machine in the first place!"

The NASA director set down the pen he had been dawdling with. "The CIA are already moving out from Sol to Andromeda. What do you say?"

"The sacrifice of many is worth the life of one," said the girl.

"Terrifying thought," a NASA doctor interjected.

"We go nova tomorrow!" the NASA director declared.

Airships glided over the riches and the squalor of Old New York City, with its gleaming television advertisements and glowing, spanning towers. Pollution darkened the dusk sky orange. It was not the ending, nor hardly a beginning, but in-between. There would be other solutions for another day, as stars hung in eternity, and possibility was more vast than we can imagine. A fat hobo, quite drunken by now, purchased a hot dog by the docks with forged money and lavished it with saurkraut, relish, hot mustard, and ketchup. In a triumphant flare, Sol burst in nova,

The prime minister, Dr. Olred, bowed and kissed the signet ring of King Vortigern VIII. "There is activity in the heavens," said the doctor, explaining his presence.

The king was somewhat wearied, at the moment, of the astrological.

"Oblige us with your observances," the king very politely enquired.

"A star on the Outer Rim has novaed prematurely," stated the counselor.

King Vortigern sprang up out of his throne. "These are very serious charges! Was it us?"

"No, m'lud, it was not us. The Society for Creative Forensics is investigating every trail, but so far find only the natives responsible. It would seem they were about to abrogate their Prime Directive." The counselor stroked his long white beard and mustache.

King Vortigern sank back down again. "Well, God damn!" he exclaimed.

Dr. Olred proceeded to the Council of Elders, where they were deep in a heated discussion. Dr. Arbuthnot was holding court in green and purple robes. "We must start investigating locally with our greatest arsenal," he stressed.

"That's a highly offensive move," Professor Belltower pointed out.

Dr. Olred, who had not been noticed entering, stood beside his chair: "The only safe thing to do is nova ourselves," he pointed out.

"That's insane!" a number of elders put in.

"Well, then, we'd be on the wanted list," Dr. Olred supplied.

"That's deranged," explained Professor Belltower.

"When all other possibilities are eliminated, the one that remains must be the truth," replied Dr. Olred. He exited the chambers to make his ablutions in secret.

Sherman sat by his telescope morosely, then hobbled with his cane over to "D" unit, where the prince and the princess were playing, to make his final report before retirement. They looked up with shining eyes and bright smiles as he entered. But he was somber.

"There is an emergency. All of Canis Minor has detonated. It may be a trans-galactic superpowers doing."

The prince and princess ceased laughing. "Oh, my God," she exclaimed. "Could such a thing be?" It was a warm day, but a cool breeze came through the window.

"The theory of trans-galactivity is evident even in ancient carvings. And certainly the rumor of a fate worse than death," Sherman said.

"Let's be reasonable," said the prince.

"It is too dangerous to be reasonable," stated Sherman.

"That's insane," the prince commented dejectedly.

Solar flares proceeded across the galaxy. Far away, Chief Engineer Phelps was high in an antechamber of the castle, reporting to the emperor.

"But who would do this but us?" the emperor stammered.

"There just may be a greater civilization than ours," supplied Phelps.

"Well, the time has come to destroy as many galaxies as possible..."

"And then perhaps ours..." thought Phelps.

CHAPTER NINE:
Visita Interiora Terrae

To say that I had been an elitist was an understatement. I cared little for the rest of humanity, and toyed with the life of a playboy. The cost of the Bridge Suite at the Atlantis Hotel and Casino in the Bahamas meant little to me, a mere twenty-five thousand dollars a night. Much of this was paid for by my usual extraordinary fortune at the gaming tables, frankly earned by counting cards and making high bids. The maximum was ten thousand dollars a hand. Women of all types were at my disposal, but this night I preferred solitude, and sipping cinnamon liquer with gold flakes. My family fortune that I had so luckily been born into was the Chiltern Valley Winery and Brewery, by appointment to Her Majesty Queen Elisabeth II. But all this wasn't enough for me, I had an outstanding goal: to cheat death itself. Here is the unlikely, yet true, account of how I managed this.

I was quite tipsy one night, and was proceeding to the casino through the ornate filigreed lobby, when an elderly, impeccably dressed Italian gentleman was seemingly entering cardiac arrest. While others gaped, I stepped to the fore, and proceeded to pound on his chest. But the attack could not be dispelled. The elderly man gripped my lapels, and whispered, nearly with his last breath, a meagre sentence in Latin: "Visita interiora terrae," he whispered, gasping for air, and then withdrew a folded envelope from his vest pocket, which he pressed into my hand. Then he was gone.

I slipped the envelope hastily into my own vest pocket, and wiped the sweat from my brow with a kerchief. I stood up before the crowd about us: "He's gone," I said, without sorrow. Hotel security arrived, and I faded into the casino for the bar. I briefly checked my platinum pocket-watch. It read ten after midnight, a time for superstition. I carefully unfolded the envelope after ordering a vermouth. It contained a single dry parchment marked only by a single curious sigil: a circle in gold ink, cut through vertically by a wavy line, and with a single dot outside the circle and a single dot inside the circle. The parchment nearly crumbled in my hands.

With my keenest insight, I realized my quest had been laid before me, I was one of the luckiest men alive. I ceased to be interested in the various ladies of the night, or even drinking. My life entered an entire reformation, my every fibre was consumed with seriousness, the graal placed before me in my very hands, purifying my spirit. I left the bar presently, and took the sole elevator up to the Bridge Suite which spanned the two towers, to immediately pack my luggage. I paid my bill with an emminently respectable credit card, and kept my cash, which I would continue to hoard so long as the quest would last.

I went home to London, and there I embarked upon a course of research, using my computer and the British Library. I meandered through antique maps, NASA photographs, and the records of the noted polar explorer Admiral Byrd. The words "visita interiora terrae" echoed in my mind, yet ultimately what I was left with was the single parchment. Years went by without conclusive deduction, but I hoarded my wealth carefully, ever so carefully, changing my habits from indulgence to asceticism. Finally, one foggy day, I discovered my unique symbol scrawled in pen on a wall near a Scottish Rite Masonic Temple. I rang the bell, but nobody answered. I continued to search through the available documents and at last came to my conclusion: a solo expedition to the Atacama Desert in Chile was necessary. I produced my living will, just in case, and ended up in the desert hill country, far from the rest of humankind. While once I had preferred the company of others, now I took to a complete and utter solitude. I wandered amongst fallen boulders, searched penetratingly into cracks and crevasses, and would not give up. A number of times I was forced to rejoin society and replenish my meagre supplies.

At last, finally, even after I entered into middle-age after years upon the quest, I discovered above a barren plain my singular answer: there, carved roughly into a large boulder, was my symbol: a circle divided by a wavy line, with one dot within the circle and another without. And there, next to the boulder, was a tumble of bricks.

The sun beat down upon me. With a racing tension I steadily removed brick upon brick, and entered a cavern in these remote mountains. Confronting me first, and unnerving me, were three mummies wrapped in brocaded, hand-dyed llama wool. I hurried past to the back of the cavern, and found my desire, the object of my search: a steep, jagged, carven stairway descending into the abyssal dark. With combined relief and anticipation I donned my backpack of provisions and employed my electric torch as a guide.

I had to pause many times, as I journeyed within the Earth itself, barely fathoming my fortune or what may lie ahead. Miles and miles passed in the torch-lit dark of the passageway, and eventually I became somewhat impeded by ancient stalagtites and stalagmites, and the way became slippery with dripping water, from which I refilled my canteen.

Days went by, until I nearly lost count. But at last a gleaming sunlight broke in front of me. I clambered out of the ancient passageway into a verdant meadow, bedeckled with greeting flowers. I could hardly contain my excitement. I first removed my spectrometer and deduced the glowing orb was yellow like our sun on the outside, but blue within. I traversed the meadow to a running stream, emiting from a spring in the hillside. Along its banks stood giant Sycamore trees, long since extinct on the surface. I faced them joyfully, but then realized my danger on my quest for immortality. What other forms extinct on the surface might be lurking? I unsheathed my automatic rifle to be on the safe side.

There it appeared, swooping from the forest, a giant pterodactyl. I aimed immediately, and fired several rounds. Marksmanship I had learned early, and it plummeted to ground.

This was fortuitous, as my provisions were nearly depleted. I roasted the rough carcass and had my fill, then pressed onwards across the spreading meadowland.

A structure appeared in the distance. It had snaking steel buttresses and crushed quartz crystal cones, but was densely overgrown, and clearly abandoned.

I entered with sheer amazement, confronted by rusted and dust-covered consoles. Then I came to one which was still lit. But its hieroglyphs gave me no clue to its use or signifigance. I decided to press onwards.

Soon I found amidst the growning grasses a path that could be seen to be worn. This I followed for many miles, and eventually I reached a lagoon. But a pack of komodo dragons were lounging on the beach, so I headed to an outcropping of stone for better vantage. I found there, to my good fortune again, a thicket of bamboo. I decided to risk building a raft, to attempt to cross this inland sea, despite the risk of sea-monsters.

The sun never moved as I worked. With some doing, I jerry-rigged a complete bamboo raft. But then, high above, a saucer-shaped craft flew rapidly overhead across the sea. I had my direction, and without further adieu placed my bamboo craft upon the waters and used a palm frond to paddle along. I now understood where the legendary flying saucers came from, not from outer space but the Earth's core.

I whistled aloud to myself as I paddled, and paused briefly to fish, but found I did not need to, as part of a school of flying fish landed on my raft. I chewed hungrily, but my much greater relish was in the discoveries that lay ahead. Dreams and fantasies flashed through my mind.

My life as an elitist had ended completely. I now merely possessed my old travel trousers, a button-down shirt and jacket, and a beaten travel hat. On the surface, I knew, my family and friends must be wondering what had become of me. But our civilization, except for books, held only discontent for me. I was on the penultimate adventure, like the graal knight returning to Camelot after his quest. My life was now full of infinite promise.

My streak of good fortune would maintain. I, Johnson Johnson, am the luckiest man in the world. A purple zeppelin floated in the distance headed in my direction. I was hailed in English: "Ahoy!" the first mate cried. "The waters are not safe, don't you know?" A rope ladder was dangled for my benefit, and I climbed aboard.

I was just in time for a pink champagne brunch with assorted delicious appetizers, among a varied crowd, all human but of different races, some in majestic robes and turbans, others in tailor-made formal dress, and even a lone fakir in loincloth in a corner, absorbed in a portable computer. But it was the women I noticed most, not one of them was not a jewel of great beauty. The first mate introduced himself as Alexander. "Glad we found you," he stated. "You're not suicidal, are you? No one goes to the park, or sails on the open sea. Are you not well?"

"I think just a touch of epilepsy," I feinted.

"Well, feel free to mingle. Here are the keys to room '7.'" Lucky number sven, I thought. This was my first glimpse of paradise, and I was hungry for more. A waiter passed by balancing a tray of pink champagne. I took two, breaking my rule.

Evidently, work was not mandatory, but it was expected that most people live in the service of others, and the people accepted. This was a far cry fom my former life as an esquire of the upper class, expecting others to live for me while I did not really gain anything. Upon this thought I receded to my quarters to meditate. They were done in tasteful off-whites and reds, with a feather mattress to rest upon. I nearly fell over, and sank into a deep sleep. But as REM took hold of me I dreamed I was flying towards a great pyramid, which contained many mysteries and treasures, and deep within, lying upon an ornate divan, was my wife. Due to this lucid dream I awoke early, and knew what I wanted to be: I wished to collect butterflies. I had never occupied a real profession until then.

I sat comfortably, the others oblivious to my presence, in the state-room, sipping cognac, when I spied our destination. Below lay the City of the Temples.

Eventually, the sadhu, the fakir I had noticed earlier, approached me in his red turban and loincloth and sandals, carrying his portable computer under one arm. He wore thick glasses on his hawk nose, which made his luminous eyes glow darkly. He peered at me intently, and said, "Don't ever try and do what is impossible for you." I immediately thought of my dream of my future wife. "It's written all over your face," he declaimed. I greatly desired discussion with him, but he left as quickly as he had come. I decided not to finish my cognac.

We hovered at last over an island with a shining city of polished marble, with walled byways and shining temples, despersed among obelisks and spires. We landed upon a quay behind a great levee. Above floated many smaller zeppelins, and balloons, and whizzing overhead was the occasional saucer like I had seen before, whose destination was a fantastically great pyramis that stood at the center of the island, upon the hill. I disembarked with wonder, and the sunlight shining in my eyes. I was met by a comely young woman driving an electric rickshaw. "Cross my palm with silver, mister?" came the old adage. I could not discern at all the genetic descent of this Gypsy.

"To the center," was my decision. I was rested and fed, and there was no time to waste. Except, on the way, I ducked into a specialty shop and bartered my rifle for a butterfly net. For the drive in the rickshaw, I gave my last gold bullion.

The pyramis rose above me, a tremendous, consummate labor of sand-stone, with four massive portals, one on either side, to allow space for the flying saucers to land.

I turned to a passerby, and enquired what they were doing. He looked at me squarely, and said, "Who doesn't know? They bring supplies of great reiches from all over the Empire for the Temple of the Empress." I then realized of the wife I had seen in my dream.

"The empress...who is she?" I dared continue.

"You had better see a doctor," the swarthy man put plainly, and went on his way hauling sage.

"How do I get an audience?" I beckoned after him.

"Only with the finest gift!" he cried as he descended a stairwell down the island.

That evening, I checked myself into a spiritual residence, which, in exchange for my room and board, put me to work scrubbing floors. This I did almost greedily. This was only the beginning, I thought.

Over the next few months I labored on building oak caskets for the assembled monks to brew with, and showed them the finest method for brewing hops. These things I had learned as heir to the Chiltern Valley Winery and Brewery, by appointment to Her Majesty Queen Elisabeth II. Now I wished to be by appointment to the empress of this exotic realm, a realm which lived in a working peace and harmony. I was rewarded for my efforts with paper credits printed with pictures of the empress herself, and my mission became more dear yet.

When I had fulfilled my mission as brewer, I was rewarded with a small plot of land behind the monastary. I constructed a plexiglass geodesic dome, and with my butterfly net proceeded to roam about the many gardens, large and small, of this beautiful island, hunting butterflies in the sun that never set. I met many people who I wished to ingratiate myself upon for conversation, but the usual response was brief, except to ask how my butterfly collection was progressing. I found swallowtails of all sorts, whitewings, longwings, ladies, red admirals, viceroys, and, of course, monarchs. I carefully netted them and released them in my modest dome, where I had planted many flowers for them to take nectar from. I would make the empress the most royal gift I could for my audience.

But it turned out I didn't have to, for rumor of my endeavors had preceded me, and after six months of steady collecting the empress herself visited my humble dwelling to see the results. She was carried on a divan, and ladies-in-waiting were fanning her with palm-fronds in the perpetual heat. She was tall, with a stately nose and wide-set green eyes, and dangling strawberrry-blonde hair cascaded down her shoulders. She wore a most simple dress of linen, but was bedecked by a plethora of rare jewels, saphires dark blue and rubies red, and a diamond necklace and royal diamond tiara. Her skin was a smooth flushed pink, and her lips full, and flushed as well.

Without a known form of appropriate address, I bowed low and said, "You honor me, m'lady."

She waved dismissively, and lightly laughed. "You may call me Uma," she responded, "Mother Goddess" as I remembered from my study of Sanskrit at Cambridge.

"Johnson Johnson," I myself replied, feeling entirely insufficient. But I remembered myself. "I have here butterflies for the royal gardens, m'lady Uma."

"Indeed. A handsome gift. Will you honor us at tonights banquet?"

I gratefully accepted. The graal had come home to Camelot. The shadow of Mordred was a thing of the distant past, after all my efforts I was finally purified. Analysis was banished, replaced by poetry, and my soul was fed.

I tripped lightly several hours later up steep stairs by a narrow sluice of running water, bordered by giant sprouting daffodils, in a large plastic cache my collection of butterflies, glowing with radiant colors.

However, at that hours revelry I was not seated near the empress, but I pressed forward momentarily to make my offering. The empress raised her jewelled hand for silence. "Let us honor our friend with the strange name," she pronounced. "And," she continued, "what part of the realms are you from?"

I froze at this. But I chose honesty. "London," I answered, now feeling completely insufficient.

"Ah?" said Uma with deep reflection. "A surface-dweller, you say?" The alternative was that I was a liar or a madman. "We have not seen one for centuries here. Are you well?" she queried penetratingly.

She was untouchably virgin, I deduced. And I had a slim chance to face my reckoning, to decide the one matter of the graal unanswered. "In exchange for the butterflies, m'lady, can you grant me my chief boon?"

She deduced this without thought. "Here, we all live forever," her stately presence declared.

This is how I gained immortality.

Years later, I sat by a London overpass watching the cars speed by, emiting their exhaust into an already polluted air. I had managed to collect a few more butterflies. The sun was now barely a speck sneaking through brown clouds made orange. A half-hour later my saucer landed in the dark. We sped past Royal Air Force jets to the North Polar Opening.

I confided to the driver as though it were a taxi, or he was a bartender. "I've decided to become a monk," I said. He adjusted his turban and said nothing.

CHAPTER TEN:
The Last Hope

A hobo lay on a park bench, asleep under a pile of newspapers. When he awoke, he skimmed through an old edition of the "The Daily Degenerate." On one of the last pages was the improbable, yet true, story of how the galaxy was nearly saved from Death Itself. It was titled "Death Is What We All Must Come To If We Live Long Enough."

Once upon a time, in the far distant past, the Milky Way galaxy was dominated by a star-spanning empire ruled by the iron fist, and stylish leather gloves, of the Emperor Thanatos himself. For the good of the Empire, individuals were "terminated" when "their time was up," or the Chief Magistrate decided they were useless to society. One of the most useless of them all was Matthew Killjoy, our hero, a parentless orphan who never removed his space-suit and helmet to reveal his true identity, just in case, although in fact it made him stand out like a sore thumb. He had fled in his modest rocket-craft to a distant star on the rim of the galaxy.

He had never worked in his life, and so was on top of the "most useless" list, and wanted by every bounty hunter in the galaxy. The posters read: "Degenerate Wanted."

He trudged along in his space-suit and helmet across the great expanse of glaciers that covered the planet. Through the blizzard, he could just descry a little light winking. He struggled towards the light.

He rarely spoke. But now, he swore: "By all the gods, and stuff!" He was unused to hearing his own voice. After all, the walls have ears, and who could you trust in these dark times? You couldn't even trust yourself, everything was so suspicious.

Matthew Killjoy reached the humble saloon after what felt like an eternity of snow and thirst. The blinking neon sign read "Last Chance Saloon." He walked through a heavy drift and forced the door open. All was dim inside, and smelt of spilt beer. Nobody cleaned anymore, it was useless. The hovel consisted of a short bar and a pool table. To his relief there was only one diminutive troll at the bar. Evidently, he thought to himself, he had not been followed. It certainly didn't look like a bounty hunter.

Matthew Killjoy sidled up to the unshaven bar-keep, who scowled and glared at him. "Two ampules of your finest vodka, hold the lime," he heard himself say mechanically.

"We're out of stock," the bartender growled. "We've got potato mash..."

"Two of those, then, hold the mash," he replied.

"Your a long way from home," the troll chuckled obviously. Killjoy did not respond. "Termination list, eh?"

"Just sight-seeing," Killjoy replied.

"I'm just sight-seeing, too," the diminutive troll lied. "Home-world is no place to be, eh?"

"It's a nice place to visit, but I wouldn't want to live there," Killjoy returned, briefly wondering at the bounty on the trolls head. In this dark age, everybody was suspicious, and many were under suspicion.

"Isn't everywhere," said the troll. "My name's Mike," he lied.

Killjoy looked implacable in his helmet. "Leibowitz," he lied. It was not a very good one.

"Whatever you say," said "Mike" the troll. "Say, listen, you seem like a reasonable man...my snow-mobile got stuck in a drift. I could use a lift, if you've got one."

There was a long pause, which turned into a very long pause. Going in groups only raised even more suspicion, and this troll already knew too much, having laid eyes on Killjoy. Still, the troll might prove to be useful, despite his overt mannerisms, and Killjoy needed a friend. "My rocket's thataway," he finally replied, gesturing vaguely. In actuality, he didn't think he could locate the rocket again in the blizzard. "What's in that direction?" he queried.

"More snow," Mike said. "But there is a single space-port. It's usually deserted, except for some dancing girls who never dance. Still, only 50 credits to teleport. Now, is it a deal?" The troll just knew he was in for the ride of his life. And friends were hard to come by, as usual.

Again there was a long pause, until: "If you've got 100 credits..."

"You drive a hard bargain," Mike replied, "but it's a deal." Matthew Killjoy seemed entirely impassive in his helmet and suit. "Hey," the troll continued, "you look like the heroic type. I happen to know a planet with a beautiful princess that needs saving...all we need is some magic..." Killjoy was trying desperately to avoid detection anywhere in the Milky Way, and nobody could yet cross the inter-galactic void. Magic might be the answer, he conjectured. He had no real talents, only flaws.

Neither party tipped the bar-keep, though both were tipsy. Later that evening, they left Earth.

It was the far distant past, and the Milky Way was about to be wracked by changes few could predict. Coincidence had generated an "Improbability Field." The Grim Reaper himself would be tested.

The pair had teleported safely for 100 credits, but had landed on Betelgeuse in the middle of a battlefield. Two races of elves were making war for the fate of the planet. Swords hacked away at each other, and arrows and javelins flew through the air. In the misty background stood a tall castle keep, which rose, sinister, spire upon spire into the sky, like an evil wedding-cake.

"All I've got is my dagger!" Mike the troll cried.

"I've got a pen-knife," replied Matthew Killjoy, fumbling in the pocket of his space-suit, "and some bubble-gum wrappers..."

"Crouch low and run," advised the troll. He was already less tall than most of the weapons. They raced towards the castle keep, and made it clear of the battlefield.

"Don't forget me!" a voice spoke, seemingly from nowhere.

"Who speaks?" dared the troll.

"Down here, on the ground." It was a short sword made of platinum and gold, with foreign runes on its blade.

"A talking sword!" exclaimed the troll. "This might come in handy!"

"I am seeking my destiny!" the sword declared.

"Then you're coming with us," Mike the troll replied. "We are destined," he added. Really he was just along for the ride. They arrived at the great castle gateway unharmed.

"Who goes there, that make their way as heroes through such battle? Fiend or foe?" said the gatekeeper.

"We have come to parley," said the sword. "We would have audience."

Matthew Killjoy and Mike the troll had really wanted to say they were on the same side, but the sword had spoken first. Mike reacted on his feet.

"As a token of good faith, we have brought the Prince this magic sword," he said. There was a long pause, like a doctors waiting room. The gatekeeper finally came to a decision.

"You may enter," he said.

"Worked like a charm," Mike said aside to Killjoy.

"You are my new owners," quoted the sword. The pair, as they waited for the gate to be drawn, peered at the mystic runes on the sword. "It says 'Made in Orion,'" the sword explained.

"We've got one chance to liberate the Princess Gedulah," Mike commented. "Follow my lead."

The gate was drawn up, creaking cryptically on its chains. "Enter," the evil elf spoke. The three of them ended up in a vast audience chamber, facing the Prince Darkhold, whose mottled visage they could just discern.

The Prince knew nothing of the Empire. His planet had been over-looked, but that would change with the arrival of the trio.

"We come to parley," the magic talking sword repeated.

"Are you gods from the stars," the elf demanded, "or just on the lam?"

"In exchange," returned Killjoy, "for the Princess Gedulah, we have brought you this magic sword..."

"That is my sword. How did it escape?"

"Possession is nine-tenths of the law," Mike interposed. "You can have your sword back, in exchange for the Princess..." Matthew Killjoy just stood there, anonymous in helmet and space-suit.

"That's jolly rotten," said the sword.

"You drive a difficult bargain, you who are not of this world. But that sword is rightfully mine, and the Princess must remain in her keep forever."

"Run!" the sword cried.

"I believe you," agreed Mike the troll.

"This way," said the sword, pointing.

They fumbled up a dark, twisting staircase. It seemed to go on forever, like a bad movie, up into the sky, until they reached a solid, locked door at the very top.

"I'll do it," the sword said as Matthew Killjoy produced his pen-knife.

"At least it picks locks," Killjoy replied. He unlocked the door with some effort. Inside the keep was bare except for a beautiful dark-haired elf with olive skin and dark eyes.

"My heroes, at last," she exclaimed, not very accurately.

"Pleased to meet you," Killjoy replied, muffled somewhat by his helmet. "But we're all trapped here now, like you."

"Not to worry," the sword interjected. "I'll teleport us all to Orion. Just stand still." But Orion was part of the Empire.

The Emperor Thanatos with his infinite, putrid mind peered into the inter-stellar void for the next planet to conquer. "Betelgeuse," he mused. The heroes had left just in time.

Thanatos was like ancient ice, with a grey beard and dour expression. He never smiled, nor grinned, at most he scowled. He had bad breath. He was of an Anti-life, born long ago in space near an asteroid. He did not relish life, only Death. Yet it was expedient to his desires to keep the masses working and enslaved, until they were deemed "useless." Then he gave them death.

The Chief Magistrate entered fearfully, knowing he, too, was at risk. A persons "usefulness" was an unknown quotient, and much of the galaxy worked feverishly, and vainly, to prove useful. "We shall conquer Betelgeuse, then," the Magistrate replied to his masters unspoken command. He bowed and retreated out the door, leaving the faint hint of cologne.

Thanatos reigned, but was feeling unusually dour, and his breath was unusually sour. He could barely discern a vague hint of the "Improbability Field" being generated. He decided it was because there were few people left alive on Betelgeuse to dominate. "So it goes..." he ruminated, sipping a green absinthe. "Death already conquers..."

The Princess Gedulah was more beautiful than other women, and so had been kept in the castle keep. At last, she had been liberated. She sat with Killjoy, Mike, and the talking sword in a cheap Hotel 666 on Orion.

"I've been targeted as 'most useless,'" Matthew Killjoy finally admitted. "I'm on the lam. It's really not safe to be seen with me. And all we have is rusty tap water."

"The best defense is a good offense," the Princess Gedulah replied, "and we are already offensive. For now, I will go out with your credits," she said to Mike the troll, "and pick up a cheap lap-top computer and some tacos. As long as we make a pact, there may be strength in numbers." She turned aside again to Killjoy. "And by the way, remaining hidden in a space-suit and helmet makes you stand out like a sore thumb..."

"I know," he bemoaned disconsolately, "but the Emperors agents know the way I look, and that cannot be good. And because there are so many useless vagabonds in this area, it is a high security district. There's an agent on every corner. We're cornered. They're bound to ask questions, especially of four like us."

"I know of someone who might help," the talking sword declared. "He remains invisible, and lives not far from here, above a saloon. But he may be a secret agent..."

"We need directions," the Princess pointed out, "so we should risk it. You have saved me, so I must save you, whatever the odds. I'll be back."

She returned in a short while. "Even the agents are suspicious of the other agents," commented the Princess Gedulah.

The computer she had purchased said: "You just can't get good help these days."

"Now we are ready," the Princess declared, "to face the invisible one. We go together as a team!"

"There is strength in numbers," the computer commented, "although most of my programming has been deleted..."

The four compatriots, along with the lap-top computer, made a stealthy ascent above a saloon. The air was musty. Hardly anyone considered cleaning being "useful."

The sword guided them to an unmarked apartment. After a brief pause to gather such wits as they had, Gedulah knocked. The door creaked open on rusty hinges. Nobody was apparent. "Please do come in," came the reply.

"Honored," Mike the troll lied. They huddled in to the dim chamber, which was strewn with old newspaper clippings from "The Daily Degenerate." "We've really gone to town," Mike said aside to the others, "he must know something."

"You will all be 'most wanted' soon," commented the invisible personage. "Personally, it took me years to become invisible. Do please have a seat." They shuffled through the debris to dusty old stuffed chairs. "Thanatos is not pleased, and the Chief Magistrate must do his work," he added. There came from the air the sound of deep guzzling.

"How do you become invisible?" countered the Princess Gedulah.

"For the secret, you must give me the sword," the invisible man returned. "I have so few people to talk to these days..."

"For the sword you must tell us," put in Mike.

"That's jolly rotten," the sword said.

"It goes like this: there lies a secret cavern on Rigel, strictly guarded by a golem. Within lies the potion of invisibility. But first you must get past the golem."

"How do we do that?" queried Gedulah.

"With a talking sword," came the reply.

"Never expect life to be fair," the sword commented.

"You've been had," said the computer, "but a deal's a deal, as they say."

"We will honor our arrangement," said Gedulah, "and face the golem without the sword. After all, we have this used lap-top."

"The golem will turn me to stone with a stare," said the computer, "and I was so happy being plastic."

"Nevertheless," put in Killjoy behind his helmet. He decided to wear shades over his vizor.

"I think I get the vibe," continued the computer, "we're doomed." As they departed from above the saloon, a secret agent glanced at them suspiciously, even as he, too, was being watched, by someone being watched. The Infiltration group was composed of 1/3 males, 1/3 females, and 1/3 party officials.

The bounty on Matthew Killjoy's head was steadily increasing. The Chief Magistrate was increasingly desperate, trying to make himself "useful." Death was angry, and as usual had the final word.

Rigel was completely illegal, and strictly off-limits, by order of Thanatos himself. He kept it as an eventual menagerie, as it was replete with monsters of all kinds. Killjoy, Mike, and the Princess heard unearthly cries in the distance, and pushed each other forward to the golems lair. There it crouched, guarding a cavern with the magical potion within. It was twelve ghastly feet tall, with slime-green skin, and dripping fangs. They all knew not to look it in the eyes, which could get one stoned.

"We have come to parley," said the computer, but all it had left was comedy programming. "Your parents didn't love you," it began, "and all your best friends are turned to rocks. But you look like a reasonable man. We will offer you salvation at only 3.75 percent interest, if you give us the potion. These are not my figures I'm quoting. They're from someone who knows what he's talking about."

The golem took immediate offense. "For the potion," it considered, "you must give me the Princess. The rest of you, frankly, disgust me."

"The Princess for the potion," Mike immediately agreed. It was an age of self-interest, after all. To the Princess he explained, "Life is a one way trip."

"We'll miss you," the computer lied.

"Have this piece of bubble-gum," Killjoy offered charitably.

The deal was struck.

Matthew Killjoy and Mike the troll absconded with the magic potion of invisibility, and the computer. They headed for the home-world near the center of the Milky Way. Night was falling quickly on the galaxy, as the Emperor Thanatos had finally decided that everyone was useless. Plus, he was beginning to detect the "Improbability Field" approaching. Everyone was on assignment, strictly, to kill each other. Those with the most credits at the end won a free lounge suite, and immediate termination. Never expect life to be fair.

The improbable duo made an appointment with the Chief Magistrate, and quaffed their invisibility potion. The Chief Magistrate heard the case.

"We come seeking employment," the lap-top computer said as the only logical line, wishing it, too, was invisible. "Completely free of charge," it added as an afterthought.

"How useless are you?" came the reply. "Anybody invisible must be 'most useless.'"

"We've been had," said Mike aside to Killjoy. But there was only going forward. "We seek audience with the Emperor," he said to the Magistrate.

"For an audience, the computer," the Magistrate replied.

"I thought we were doomed," said the computer.

"For the computer, the audience," said Mike. But they were running out of gambits. They were down to a few pieces of bubble-gum.

The audience chamber of the Emperor Thanatos looked like something from the Spanish Inquisition. "This can't be good," the troll understated. "Do you have any good lines?"

The Emperor Thanatos appeared more dour than usual.

"We come seeking your Fate," said the invisible troll.

"I do not know what you are talking about," answered Death, "but I grant you a year's supply of tuna fish and immediate termination." At that moment, the invisibility potion wore off.

"Expect the unexpected," cried Matthew Killjoy. He removed his helmet, revealing himself as the Emperors only begotten son.

"You are the most useless," the Emperor commented.

"That didn't work," put in the troll.

"And he never did," replied Death. He hailed an orderly. "Two crucifixes, immediately," he commanded.

Soon Matthew Killjoy and Mike the troll were bleeding to death on crucifixes. Matthew Killjoy was trying to enjoy his last piece of bubble-gum.

Mike the troll commented: "The motto of this story is never double-cross."

"That's a terrible joke," Killjoy returned as he breathed his last on the cross, "and totally useless."

CHAPTER ELEVEN:
The Weir on the River Lethé*

* "The River of Forgetfulness," also a river in Alaska.

Dr. Joseph Nicholas Bell could not think of the formula, for the life of him. The moss-covered roof of his diminutive shack was leaking, again, and smoke was drifting in his single window. He closed the shutters, and hoped something else would remind him. It was freezing cold, but the mice were out squeaking again for table scraps. Instead of concentrating, he decided to fish at the weir. His supply of mice were precious to him. Anyhow, perhaps the meditation of fishing would bring the answer.

The water of the River Lethé flowed over the weir he had built, lo, these seventy years ago. The heavy smoke was nearly suffocating, so he pulled his woolen scarf over his mouth and nostrils. He let his rusty fish-hook sink into the waters of the weir. But no formula came. For some reason, he was unusually frustrated.

The Valley of Ten Thousand Smokes in Alaska was also unusually frustrating, the smoke much heavier than usual. He sat in the dim light, surrounded by ash, and waited. Soon he became quite hungry, but he refused to set a mouse trap. If he ran out of mice he might run out of food. He began hoping for a toad or a frog.

Finally, there was a catch. It was barely bigger than a minnow. But it tasted to him like salmon. He put a scrap on his hook. More smoke drifted through, but he guessed, correctly, that it was a false alarm. Dr. Bell was a master of forensic diagnosis. It was the case that answers came easily to him, but the back of his mind began bothering him again.

He drank from the ice-cold stream to further relieve his appetite. He could not sleep, but as he continued to fish he began falling into a hypnotic trance. This was always preferable, for relaxation, and perhaps so the singular answer might come. But he was startled into wakefulness by the tug of a frog. The mice would have something to eat, and he would have a mouse.

"I'm hungry," the mice squeaked as he entered the ramshackle hut. He tore the frog into little bits, and lured the fatter of the mice to him. There was no spare wood to burn, but with his flint-stone he lit some dried moss, seared the hair off the mouse, and devoured it hungrily.

"By George, I think I've got it," he said to no one in particular except the mice. "I'm expecting a visitor!"

There presently came a rapping at his door. He did not hesitate, but opened it expectantly. The mice scattered.

It was a tall, lean man, but clean shaven, wearing brown robes like a Jesuit. The stranger did not take back his hood, but in the dim light Dr. Bell could just descry hawk-like eyes above a hawk-like nose.

The man took a branch from his cape and extended it as a gift. "You shall have warmth tonight," he spoke almost in a whisper.

"Thank you," replied Dr. Bell, half bemused and half in alarm. He had not seen a man or had extra wood in years, but his mind was more occupied with those eyes, and where the man had gotten a clean razor for his shave. Dr. Bell sank back into his wooden rocking-chair which he had built long ago, which was padded with dry moss. "I would offer you a mouse, but they scattered in alarm..."

"Not a problem," said the tall gentleman who looked like a monk. Or a warlock, Professor Bell conjectured. "I had caribou three days ago," added the mysterious stranger. Dr. Bell was about to invite this imposing figure in, but could tell that the man would not budge from the doorway. Smoke began to drift in from the pits.

Nothing more was said for a full three minutes, as Dr. Bell counted. The figure seemed to loom taller and taller in the twilight, and for a moment seemed like he might gesticulate. But Dr. Bell quickly interrupted. "Do you have any tobacco, or a drink?" he queried. It had been years, long years, with only his papers and pencils, and mice. Caribou sounded delicious, but he dismissed that.

There was a last supply of tobacco and whisky for them both. The log for the fire could wait. Dr. Bell exerted himself to remain calm. "Have a seat, if you prefer," he said politely, gesturing to a large pile of moss, but not offering the man his rocking chair. Dr. Bell decided he would be diffident, despite the royal gifts. He briefly thought that the stranger could scavenge more caribou, but he dismissed this also. The unexpected guest had been frustrating him all day throughout his formulas, but he was ready for almost anything.

The man sat peculiarly on the moss pile, with one leg over a knee. Dr. Bell, in the fading twilight, could just discern that the man's cape had no stains of caribou blood. A clay pipe of dry tobacco was passed, and a caribou-skin flagon of whisky.

"They come tonight," the man said.

But Dr. Bell was enjoying too much to reply. The doctor noticed it was a weak moment for himself, and decided to change the subject. He concentrated acutely.

"The moon is full, and yellow," he replied in his most casual manner. Although he preferred silence, he was nevertheless expectant. He arose and closed the door, which the mysterious gentleman had not done, and enjoyed greatly the smell of tobacco instead.

"The People of the Moon will come," the stranger spoke. He seemed to have a certain respect for the doctor, as though he knew the doctor was an analyst. Not to mention, a character analyst. There was another long pause as the caribou decanter was passed between them. The doctor chose to be direct, and indirect.

"Do you prefer conversation?" he queried.

"Never touch the stuff," the stranger replied with truly unexpected humor.

Dr. Bell changed the subject. "I could smoke out a mouse..."

"There is little time. The People of the Moon will come..."

"I'm not afraid of Inuit," said the doctor, referring to the Eskimos.

The man's humor drained away. "They are from the moon, those of which I speak." The monk at last threw back his hood, to reveal close-cropped hair with no grey detectable in the growing dusk. The doctor assumed the man possessed scissors. His own had rusted away years ago, despite his best efforts. For some reason, he felt almost embarrassed by his own nearly bald head with its long strings of white. But he did not envy youth, he merely coveted wisdom. To his faint dismay, another long pause intervened. "The People of the Moon are looking for wisdom," the man said, and for a moment his dark, hawk-like eyes flashed piercingly. The doctor put some dried moss into his old fire pit, and proceeded with the log.

"Prescient," Dr. Bell thought to himself with certitude. Then he inhaled the dry tobacco as deeply as he could. His lungs were weak, from all the smoke continually outside. He gladly took another swig of whisky, and decided to relax. "And do you have a name, sir?" he asked, not forgetting his lines. It was the most pertinent question in the book: "What's in a name?" And the very first thing you usually ask a demon. Not to mention, the appellation "sir" had the unnerving ring of an insult. The monk paused.

"Osman," he stated with evident honesty. "Osman Ratchet."

"Can't say that I've heard it before," the doctor replied calmly, beginning to be much bemused. But his frustration at not finding the answer to his formula was still increasing. It had been only at the last moment that he had expected the man, and the monk was mysterious still. But not more mysterious than himself, he knew.

The odor of sulphur was beginning to dissipate at last, but the tobacco and whisky were entirely depleted. And hunger was gnawing at him again. Again, he decided to change the subject. "Do you have relations?" he jested without betraying his mirth. The log fire was glowing hot now, and the strangers face flickered like a shadow-play.

"I knew an old hermit once, but the People of the Moon came for him..."

"Are you a Jesuit?" Dr. Bell asked politely, enquiring into the brown robes.

"The caribou are restless..." came the man's reply. "They are coming soon..."

"So you said," Dr. Bell answered, pausing reflectively for a moment. He hadn't seen another human in seventy years. "Perhaps they are just curious."

"This is no game," replied the monk sternly. "Haven't you had enough?" he managed to joke. The doctor almost took a liking to him.

Suddenly, there came another rapping at the door. This surprised the doctor entirely. He was this time truly tentative, which he was unused to. But he was also tipsy and relaxed, so he decided to answer. He was nearly in another hypnotic trance. "Who is it?" he asked.

"Just open the door," came a thin voice. There was nothing else to do, so the doctor sank into relaxation and opened the door, with a terrible creaking from the rusty hinges. There stood a midget with a thin mustache, wearing a tight blue suit and thin black tie, and carrying a briefcase. "We've come to take you to the hospital," the midget declared professionally.

"You and what army?" said Dr. Bell boldly, without need of mustering himself, as he was in trance. "Or are you offering me employment?" The monk said nothing, but was fingering something in his pocket. Dr. Bell noticed, but turned to the midget.

"I'm Dr. Tandora," the midget introduced himself. "I'm a psychologist." Dr. Bell awoke from his trance. He was glad he was tipsy. "We need you for observation," the distinguished midget declared. The monk stood up suddenly, but the midget turned to him and commanded, "Steady, Osman." The monk sat back down on the moss. The room was now full of smoke, and night had settled in. "Code Grey, Bill," the midget said over his shoulder.

A strapping man strode without hesitation into the little shack, grinning. He wore a white nurses smock, but was really Vice-Admiral of the Marines. He tightly gripped Dr. Bell's arm and led him out the door.

"We're all crazy on this bus," Dr. Bell heard the monk mutter, "but better him than me..."

"See you later," the midget Dr. Tandora said to Osman Ratchet. "You're a man that knows too much!"

"There's nothing to know," came the parting reply.

"The most sophisticated hydrogen fuel cell ever! One teaspoon of water per mile!" the television blared.

"Can you change it to a soap opera?" a little old lady asked.

The 40th floor of the Presidio Hospital in San Francisco was nearly impenetrable. Dr. Bell felt fine on his Valium, but his blood pressure was high, 147 over 102, so he was on a low-salt regimen. "General Hospital" was on TV. He abandoned hope, suspecting indoctrination procedures were at work. He went to a nurse for blue Gatorade and cheese sticks.

Osman Ratchet was smoking out mice. But Dr. Bell's notes had been taken. The moon was a waning gibbous. The slim Alaskan day made him increasingly nocturnal. The weir of the River Lethé was slowly filling with small fish.

Dr. Bell peered out an enormous bullet-proof window at the San Francisco skyline. He made out first the Mark Hopkins Hotel, the tallest building in the City, and then the Hyatt-Regency with its turning restaurant on top and exterior glass elevator. Looking below, he saw Central Park West, with its ruined marble fountain and tumbled columns, left as a memorial to the Great Earthquake of the 27th century. Dr. Bell, with his intact acute memory, could recall the shaking of his old diagnostic offices on Market Street. He briefly wondered about the memory of the other patients, but especially the staff. He dearly missed his lost notes, but he had been busy in the rec room re-recording many of the essentials. He preferred his formula in front of him, not just in his head. He was old-fashioned.

He had finally gotten a shave and a trim, but had left his grey sideburns.

"Bill" the nurse (not his real name), came striding down the hall in his nurses smock and I.D. badge. This was someone Dr. Bell wanted to meet again, despite the man's superior physical prowess.

He extended his hand as he walked beside the nurse. "Hello, Bill," he offered.

"Hello, Joseph," came the reply. They shook hands with firm grips. Bill seemed on the surface without pretense, except he wore a permanent grin. "Free time is nearly over. The meeting will be in the Picasso Wing today."

"Thank you, Bill," Dr. Bell decided to say simply, "and can you get me a piece of nicotine gum?" Next time, he vowed, they would have a more complete conversation.

"Sure thing," Bill responded.

The Picasso Wing held the art room. Dr. Bell tried to immerse himself in the accepted therapy. His only hope was good behaviour. He produced a charcoal sketch of the weir on the River Lethé, his greatly missed home in Alaska. The details were almost exact, with a smoke of moss arising from the ash-rock chimney into the haze of the Valley of Ten Thousand Smokes. The culvert where his cabin lay was perfectly realized. His memory was "eidetic," or "photographic."

But then he turned his attention to a collage for the last thirty minutes. He poured through old copies of Home and Garden, Vogue, and Vanity Fair, and produced a montage of super-models surrounded by photographs of fruit. Finally, the bell tolled, and he knew he must see his doctor for the first time.

The midget Dr. Tandora sat firmly planted in a padded chair much too large for him. Dr. Bell received a small wooden chair with no arms. This was intended to establish psychological superiority for the doctor. Dr. Tandora briefly stroked his thin mustache. He held up a black ink Rorschach blot.

"Well, Joseph, what does this remind you of? You can have three impressions." Without vanity, Dr. Bell was still incensed at not being called "doctor." The

Valium was wearing off, and he was coming out of hypnos. He studied the illustration briefly. As usual, the Rorschach test contained a mirror image of an amorphous shape.

"A bat is obvious," stated Dr. Bell. "But also it could be mountains reflected in a lake. But especially it seems to be the Unconscious, reflecting itself to the Conscious." Without trance, Dr. Bell was becoming wearied. He had been in the Large Presidio Facilities South Wing for exactly eleven months, with hardly a clue. On Valium, his formula was divided in two, like a Rorschach test: two undesirable alternatives, of staying in the hospital, or worse, receiving investigative surgery. He knew the tests were running out.

"What does the Unconscious say to the Conscious?" Dr. Tandora, in his tight blue suit and thin black tie, asked pertinently.

Dr. Bell decided to make up his best response, to satisfy the therapeutic process. "The Unconscious says: 'I reflect you. I am like you. We touch, but we do not know each other. But my language is your language, and we exist within the world of symbolism.' And for every action in the one there is a corresponding action in the other. Furthermore, the Unconscious says, 'I am a Beast, and you are but a Man. I will rule over you until the End of Days, when finally one of us must destroy the other.'" The midget seemed entirely implacable, and held up one more test. This one was in color, with pinks and greens.

"The sunset over the Valley of Smokes," said Dr. Bell immediately. "But also a moth pollenating a flower. Or nuclear radiation making an orchard bloom with gigantism, with pink flowers and a green apple tree.

There is also a goat that remains hidden, who can only be detected by his horns."

"Thank you," said Dr. Tandora with no politeness. "Now I must inform you that you are ready for the East Wing. You shall have a delightful view of the bay, and the glass pyramid on Alcatraz Island. And the nurses there are female." Dr. Tandora peered at Dr. Bell with beady eyes, but could, as usual with the staff, detect no overt signals from his face, except the very faintest of smiles, despite the potential for ruin. East Wing could be Heaven, and it could be Hell. Gestapo nuns were no laughing matter whatsoever.

"Dr. Tandora," Dr. Joseph Nicholas Bell pleaded, "could you raise my dosage of Valium before I leave?"

"I've already done that. Instead of 5 milligrams you shall receive 10."

"Thank you, doctor." Dr. Bell, the oldest living human, older than Methuselah, had never had Valium until the Large Presidio Facility, and enjoyed the trance-like state very much. Plus it relieved his stress and anxiety.

He was not anti-social per se, but a creature of solitude. He knew the nuns would have no attraction for him, only, perhaps, the chaplain. "This could be Heaven, this could be Hell," he mused to himself as he left the doctor's office, to be accompanied by nurse Betsy to the East Wing. The Gestapo had revealed no clues, only minor mysteries. The Bigger Picture yet awaited.

On the East Wing the pyramid shown in the bright noonday sun. Greta the nurse approached him in the mess hall, and said, "You have an allowed visitor." It was his first, and although he could not suspect fully, he sensed that he knew this visitor personally. And he had seen only one person in the last seventy years before hospital. He was served coffee with Sodium Pentathol, or "truth serum," in it for the occasion, which would be monitored on close-circuit TV for the record.

The visitor was Osman Ratchet, who no longer wore Jesuit robes but a natty three-piece tweed outfit, with a silver chain from a pocket-watch dangling from his left vest pocket. "I came into my inheritance," he explained upon their greeting. "But I have only one year to spend, or the government will take everything. I would flee to Andorra, and work on telescopes, but I'm not allowed to leave the country. I believe I've been classified 'FM,' for 'Formerly Missing.' I left your cabin intact, let me tell you," he added, "but it, obviously, is now known."

"Do you know what became of my notes?" queried Dr. Bell.

"The People of the Moon absconded with them. Do you still have the "X" formula in your head?" This was a highly suspicious question.

"We're being monitored," replied Dr. Bell cautiously.

"You can tell me something. Just one shred of the Immortality Serum." Osman's hawk-like eyes peered at Dr. Bell as though from the heights. There ensued a lengthy pause, and the air tingled with static.

Dr. Bell thought it judicious to partially relent, both for this canny individual and potentially his money, and for those who had monitored him these last eleven months. He gazed briefly at the shining pyramid, with its four Egyptian obelisks about. He relented finally: "Ten percent serum, ninety percent water," the doctor said.

"I see," replied Osman Ratchet the Third. "Anything else?"

"Oxy-helium," the doctor let slip due to Sodium Pentathol. He took another sip of coffee. Osman Ratchet changed the subject.

"Are they giving you Valium?" he said.

"Yes. I've had many good trances," came the honest reply.

"Here is my card. If you are ever released, look me up in the Old Chronicle Building." He paused for a full minute. "One other thing: beware of nurse Greta. She's the very worst of the lot. I barely escaped Full Indoctrination Procedures when I was here." Dr. Bell automatically became sympathetic, but hopeful. But a tone sounded, indicating the ten minutes were up. "Remember: only once in a blue moon," were Osman's parting words.

"That's good advice, from someone who made it Outside," Joseph Bell answered with a sense of gratitude and humility. "Go in pieces," he decided to jest, remembering the strangers former good humor.

"Sat nam," came the salutational goodbye.

Nurse Greta opened the door. Her crinkled skin about bright blue eyes affected enmity and wrath. "Over," she declared simply. She knew she was a cog in a machine, but with preeminence. Osman departed rapidly in distaste.

"Can I have another cup of coffee?" Dr. Bell asked her, feigning innocence.

"You must wait until dinner."

The weir on the River Lethé was collecting fish. Dr. Tandora had mysteriously "disappeared," and "Bill" the nurse, Vice-Admiral of the Marines, was still grinning.

Greta Braun was Ambassador to the London Naval Consulate, a consummate spy like "Bill." Her crinkled skin had brown bags from too much Thorazine and generic menthol cigarettes. She was slightly sway-backed and emaciated.

She entered Dr. Bell's room, number 13, which he shared with another man who could not stop talking out loud (and would later die of Sudden Unexplained Death Syndrome, quicker than a heart attack). Nurse Greta approached Dr. Bell as he lay awake in bed. "I have a scheduled Morphine injection," she declared, not quite truthfully, as there was also a small amount of arsenic, which kills over time in periodic small dosages.

And time was running out, Dr. Bell knew. He could not penetrate the bullet-proof glass, he could not reach an elevator, but he had barely spied through a door a secret dumb-waiter where drugs would arrive from "D" section. He had overheard Nurse Greta: "The fifth floor made another error."

Dr. Bell had secretly been hoarding rubber cement from the art room. That very night, Friday the 13th of December, 3325 a.d., he painted his hospital skivvies heavily with rubber cement, and calmly, yet with anticipation, induced self-hypnosis. Dr. Joseph Nicholas Bell then strolled with complete, if perhaps unwarranted, confidence into the darkened atrium of the East Wing of the 40th floor. The nurses, as he knew they would be, were preoccupied with update reports in an antechamber. He gracefully sidled by the window of their door unnoticed. He came to the drug dispensary, and produced from his garments a skeleton key made from pieces of a cut plastic cup, glued together for strength. With some fiddling and fidgeting the lock gave way. He pressed the "Do Not Disturb" button on the other side of the door, and began helping himself to drugs, as swiftly as he could. Morphine, Valium, Norco 5, Ritalin, Marinol. He then pressed the "eject" button for the dumb-waiter. The small slot opened with no lift within, as he had anticipated. He squeezed himself in feet first, and with all his strength, pressing against the walls of the descent with his cement-covered garments, made his way slowly but surely towards the 5th floor. At last, he emerged into the medication storage chambers, which, as he expected, were deserted for the lunch of the night staff. It paid to be a doctor. He helped himself to more drugs by glueing the plastic bottles to his outfit, then donned a fake nurses smock he had cut out of his sheets.

He said, "Sat nam," to the night guard, an imposing Sikh, strolled through the lobby, helped himself to a complimentary coffee with non-dairy creamer, and finally skipped out the automatic sliding doors. He paused briefly for the sound of any commotion or alarms, and hearing nothing, proceeded to walk with uncontrolled elation, yet slowly, through the Presidio complex, towards the Tenderloin. He would have to sell some drugs for money. He snapped his thumb and finger before his eyes and came out of trance.

A half hour later, a night-shift nurse did a bed-check and discovered the singular English patient missing. Street lights around the City flashed yellow three times, denying municipal codes, and Gestapo shadow teams began prowling for one Dr. Bell, except for several in all-night cafes who pretended to read newspapers and waited.

Dr. Bell was busily making a mint in the Tenderloin with Morphine, Norco 5, and Marinol, as he chewed an enormous wad of nicotine gum. He quickly ceased operations with his sleazy clients, hurried to the only all-night laundry-mat he could remember nearby, and rapidly ascertained which washers were not being watched. He helped himself to a rough pair of black cotton pants and a white polyester button-down, breathed rhythmically to calm his adrenalin, and waited nervously at the nearest bus stop for a late-night. His photographic memory had not failed him.

A Central Intelligence Agency spy was on the bus, but had absolutely no way to recognize the doctor. After a brief ride, Dr. Joseph Nicholas Bell attempted to register at the Hyatt-Regency Hotel, but had no I.D. to register with. Yet, a significant bribe was sufficient, as most everybody needed money in these desperate times. He registered in room 13 on the first floor, for a sense of irony, and also as a contingency measure in case of the need for a quick escape. In the lobby was an open gift shop, where he bought that day's edition of the San Francisco Chronicle, and headed for his room to order room service. He placed a "Do Not Disturb" placard on his door-knob, then ordered orange juice and chocolate cake, as all that seemed palatable presently.

He turned on the cable TV to the NASA station, to see the latest reports from the Lunar Colonies. A new township named "Middletown" had just been established on the dark side of the moon. The Gestapo were hard at work.

A rapping came at the door. "Room service," a woman's voice proclaimed. Dr. Bell peered through the peep-hole and, with Holmesian deduction, ascertained she was innocent. He received the orange juice and chocolate cake gladly, and purchased from her cart two packs of Marlboro 100's. Life was sweet again, but only temporarily. He was deathly afraid of the Gestapo. If they could find him at the River Lethé, they could perhaps find him in San Francisco. He longed for his former solitude, but he had to lie very low and not leave the familiarity of the City. Where was there to run to? At least, the tortoise had beat the hare.

For the Gestapo, or its remnants, it seemed that world domination was no longer the issue, but world destruction. The Fourth Reich, he ascertained, were preparing to live on the moon, and from there prepare the destruction of earth. The People of the Moon, he further ascertained, would use neutron bombs, thereby destroying the population of earth but let buildings stand, so that they could, eventually, re-colonize. Yet he also thought he knew that ultimately, in their hierarchy, the Gestapo could not trust each other, with double and triple agents being possible, especially the psychics. This might be used to his advantage. He had found a new mission.

He did not go out that day, nor the next, but sat watching television and taking spas in his suite. But then plans had to be enacted. If necessary and possible, he would use Osman Ratchet for more money.

The first thing he did was to creep out early one morning, with a complete haircut and shave. Suspicious characters seemed everywhere, so he hired a Yellow cab to take him to the Industrial District, and then to a tailor. Back at his suite, he prepared prosthetics. He made his slim frame paunchy and gave himself a double chin and heavy bags under the eyes. He then went back to the Tenderloin, newly dressed in a grey three-piece and red bow-tie, and, after much negotiating, accessed the black market, and purchased for his brown eyes green contact lenses which could foil a retinal scan. He would make a journey to the moon. But first, he knew he must kill "Bill" the nurse, the most glaringly suspicious of the lot.

The Old Chronicle Building had for the last millennia-plus been luxury suites. It had survived the earthquakes. Dr. Bell peered out Osman's window disconsolately. "I must kill Bill," he confessed.

Osman's hawk-like features were attentive. "I've thought so, too. He's involved no matter how you look at him." He went to his mahogany desk and withdrew a Smith and Wesson with a silencer. "No matter how you look at it, he has to commute to work. Champagne?"

"A toast," declared Dr. Bell, "to the long war against bigotry and hatred!"

"You have my very best wishes, and my sympathies. I myself, too, must disappear, then. I shall return to the weir on the River Lethé, and await you hopefully there..."

Dr. Bell withdrew an envelope from his vest. "These are my surviving notes, for you to keep and read."

"I'm honored. I shall wait for a special time," Osman replied. He slipped six unmarked bullets into the pistol. "Good luck, as the Gypsies say!"

"One other thing," Dr. Bell queried. "May I have your pocket-watch? I'm a hypnotist..."

"Gladly. I had it monogrammed 'Oz.'"

"Perhaps we'll get over the rainbow yet. We must keep the Tin Woodman's heart beating..." This was a fine toast.

They clinked glasses and drank, so it would come true.

"Bill" the nurse commuted every day from the FMC (Federal Military Consulate) to the Presidio Hospital by unmarked police cars. His strapping muscular frame and murderous grin were clearly visible in the early dawn, on New Year's Day. He exited the black vehicle in his nurses smock after a long night at work. It was a dangerous place for a murder, outside the Presidio Hospital.

Dr. Bell rode by in his prosthetics and a baggy grey jump-suit on an antique bicycle. "You're going to Sheol," he whispered to the dragon. The car drove off, and Dr. Bell put six unmarked, silent bullets into Bill's head, and rode off smiling in the opposite direction. He threw the gun down a sewer grate.

Dr. Tandora's whereabouts were unknown, but Greta the nurse soon learned of the event. She rang the London Naval Consulate and screamed, "I quit!" She then went to the Director of Hospital Staff and said, "That's it!" She was headed for the moon.

Interpol caught wind of the events, and enquiring minds wanted to know. The KGB soon learned, but they were the Gestapo. Plans began to accelerate. For every action, an equal and opposite reaction.

It began to rain, for forty days and forty nights. Bill's body was cremated and placed below the Lincoln Memorial.

The patients at the Presidio Hospital were quarantined indefinitely, as more organizations began to investigate. But neither Dr. Bell's nor Bill's trail could be followed.

Cal-tech in the Pyrenees, between France and Spain, was launching another balloon to test the ozone layer again in the upper stratosphere. Dr. Bell learned of it on the NASA channel back at the Hyatt-Regency. He had switched his prosthetic molds to that of an angular young man, complete with toupee and a real dyed mustache, which he waxed. Fortunately, he never sweated. The rain beat against his window. The murder never made it onto TV, by agreement never to publish anything detrimental to national security. But the Chronicle read: "Presidio Hospital Quarantined Indefinitely." Many people wished to get in, a first in history. Everybody inside wanted to get out. Only Greta Braun had escaped, with her Thorazine and generic menthols, except for Dr. Tandora, who was still missing.

Dr. Bell crept out of the Hyatt-Regency at 3 a.m., January 2nd, boarded an armored black limousine truck, and headed to the San Francisco Airport for the Concorde 500. Time was of the essence. It was the bus trip from Paris that was the lengthy procedure, especially as they didn't allow smoking.

"Monsieur Proust," he introduced himself to the Legal Secretary at Cal-tech, twirling his waxed mustache. "Is the Director of Operations in?'

"Potentially," she replied, with the strong hint of a hint. He paid her in gold bullion.

"You want to board our balloon in this weather?!" the man exclaimed incredulously.

"I am seeking God," Dr. Bell lied. A greater sum of gold bullion was paid, especially for silence.

Dr. Bell's tiny balloon was pummeled by the stratospheric cumulus, as it passed into the upper atmosphere. He threw out the extra weight of the ozone detector.

Dr. Tandora sat quietly in a Nazi safe house in Argentina. "I'm going to Middletown," he stated simply. Various satellites began to change their positions.

Dr. Bell was donning his Kevlar suit and jet-pack. The clouds shown below him. An oxygen tank and helmet were also required. He shot towards the People of the Moon.

The mice were well-fed at last. Osman Ratchet was standing by the weir, looking up at the dark, smokey sky. He knew the moon was there, closer or further, non-spheroidical, mottled.

The moon has more than 4000 gravitational influences upon it. Dr. Bell was busily combining algorithms. He desisted his jet-pack precisely six feet above the lunar surface, and floated harmlessly down. He knew he had to hitch a ride. Middletown awaited in the dark.

The first vehicle to come around was luckily unoccupied. It was a modest tractor in the form of a geodesic dome, with six wheels. Luckily, it seemed to be headed in the right direction. Perhaps it was Gypsy luck that would defeat the Gestapo. Luck was not to be underestimated, Dr. Bell knew.

He climbed aboard, and out of curiosity cut an incision into the plastic dome. As luck would have it, the dome contained cigarettes and another oxygen tank. It also had a small homing device and radar so as to reach their destination. However, luck is a thing that might run out, and Dr. Bell knew full well that radar and magnetic imagery might detect him before he reached the settlement. He also left a heat signature.

The small transport vehicle took him over a dusty path, through asteroid craters and finally through the mountains. The Vetruvius Crater was left in the gloam, and the vehicle skirted Mons Vetruvius and found a track through the mountains.

The humble new settlement of Middletown had been built by machine and had few amenities. But there was a docking port into the arcade complex, which was in the shape of a pentagon. A door slid open before him, and he debarked into a decontamination unit. He removed his Kevlar suit and his oxygen tank and helmet, down to his stylishly cut grey three-piece and red bow-tie. He allowed a syringe to draw blood so he could pass, and with his black market contact lenses passed the next procedure. A screen briefly flashed: "Free of disease. Iridology lower class. Press here to review Terms of Acceptance."

He lit a cigarette. No alarm had sounded. In fact, no one was manning surveillance. The only other people in Middletown were nurse Greta Braun and the midget psychologist Dr. Tandora, and they were locked in the adytum of a small Scottish Rite masonic temple, preoccupied with delicately handling uranium for a Sprint warhead. Dr. Bell already suspected something of the sort.

Meanwhile, he found a Motel 6 and watched reruns and waited. He had his own master weapon, donated by Osman Ratchet, but he must negotiate for some uranium to activate his own deadly device. He reflectively lit another cigarette, and sank into deep analysis. What could be relied upon?

The television showed him a map of the settlement. There was one all-night cafe manned by androids, a small pharmacy, a dorm, one public restroom, and the temple. It was an easy deduction where the other inhabitants were, the adytum behind the altar. After all the peaceful ages of mankind, a further crucible must be met. Dr. Bell had not arrived too soon, from the Valley of Ten Thousand Smokes and the Presidio Hospital.

He casually walked out of his room, "lucky number 13," and strolled lightly to the Scottish Rite temple, entered into the Egyptological bas-reliefs of the main center of ritual, slipped behind the altar, and knocked on the door of the adytum. He withdrew his pocket-watch, monogrammed "Oz."

Room service!" he yelled loudly. There was no response. "Special delivery!" he tried again. "2=0!" he shouted finally. At this, he could just hear some commotion, as the residents of the adytum were sealing documents and vials of uranium into a safe behind a painting of Baphomet, god of the Templars. The wooden door swung open, and there appeared the hideous, dotted, crinkled visage of Greta Braun.

"'Delenda Carthago,' the Great Cato said," cried Joseph Bell in his disguise. "Is Carthage greater than Rome?"

"This means war!" spat Miss Braun.

Dr. Bell dangled the silver pocket-watch before her eyes. "But you are feeling sleepy..."

"I am feeling sleepy," she admitted. His voice had a particular intonation.

"Watch the watch, and think back to when you were a little child..."

"I was a Hitler Youth," Miss Braun admitted.

"Further back, when you slept so well. Imagine a bath full of bubbles, and your first toy..."

"It was a water-pistol..." she admitted.

Dr. Tandora's voice came thinly from within: "Don't listen!"

But the hideous Greta Braun was anesthetized, as sure as with Chloroform. Dr. Bell placed a plastic bag over her head and tied it off with a piece of yarn.

Dr. Tandora sat behind an ebony desk in his tight blue suit and thin black tie, with his thin mustache twitching and his beady eyes staring.

Dr. Bell entered. "Never try to second-guess a second-guesser," he stated simply, thus creating a new proverb.

"My apartment, as you can see it," came the cautious reply from the midget.

"Appearances can be deceiving," said Dr. Bell, immediately noticing everything with his photographic memory and dark retinal lenses hidden by his contacts.

Dr. Tandora peered into the console on his desk at the x-ray. "You are wearing prosthetics. Who are you?" he queried somewhat desperately: it was the age-old question and game, "what's in a name," and the first question you ask a demon. Dr. Tandora was caught between the proverbial rock and the hard place: should he destroy this man, or wait to gain more information.

Dr. Bell twirled his dyed, waxed mustache. "I am Monsieur Proust," he lied, "King of the Gypsies," he added for good measure. He himself was buying time.

"Dr. Tandora's reply was immediate: "I have here a button to destroy you with. Tell me what I want to know!"

"You have acid reflux, and cataracts. And you've recently undergone a spinal tap, as you know. But additionally, you are experiencing no loss of bone density from outer space, whose function I am unaware of. You had an additional pair of wisdom teeth removed. You are mildly jaundiced from alcohol intake, indicating the need for kidney and liver tonics. You were not happy as a child because you felt inferior, and ever since you have been attempting to negate this by gaining power."

"Stop!" Dr. Tandora commanded. The two doctors merely looked at each other for a few moments.

"Parlez-vous Francaise?" Dr. Bell inquired. He had observed everything in the apartment he needed to know. "Viva la France!" he cried. "Now, hand over the Baphomet!"

Dr. Tandora was producing a ruby laser, but Dr. Bell had already surmised the other doctors patience quotient. He expertly flung two darts, one to each eye.

Dr. Tandora collapsed in genuine agony, and began writhing on the lead floor.

Dr. Bell immediately removed the painting of Baphomet, and threw it across the room. He examined the dial on the safe, which had digits up to two hundred. "'666' is too obvious," he said out loud. "What would a Nazi do?" This was a stumper. He thought through objective and subjective number variants. Five minutes passed, then ten. But he did not sweat. "What would a Nazi do?" He reviewed dozens of mathematical riddles. "By George, I think I've got it! A Nazi would fib. Fibonacci!" he declared loudly for no one. "That's easy!" He greased his fingers on his mustache so as not to leave finger-prints. "Fibonacci Numbers!" He began turning the dial of the safe. "Zero, 1, 1, 2, 3, 5, 8, 13, 21, 34, 55, 89, 144! That's it!" The door slid open heavily.

As fast as he could, Dr. Bell removed the vials of uranium. Satellites, he knew, must be moving into position. From a vest pocket he withdrew a small box, Osman's gift: sycamore wood on the outside, steel on the inside. The box glowed with a soft, purple-blue aura.

Dr. Bell prepared with great alacrity for his final moments. He placed a vial of uranium within the box. "Ram!' he said with his dying breath, the highest god-name in Hinduism, so that he might reincarnate.

Oranur radiation spread out across the moon, turning it burnt sienna with deadly clouds of luminiferous ether. Every living thing on the moon proceeded to die.

Osman Ratchet was fishing at the weir of the River Lethé in the Valley of Ten Thousand Smokes in Alaska. It was full of fish as small as minnows. The dim sunlight shown through, and a light breeze was carrying the smoke in the opposite direction. He said mildly to his Inuit companion, Akkikiktok, "Dinner will be ready soon."

Three days later there came a rapping at the door again. Osman opened it without hesitation.

It was the Executive Director of the Presidio Hospital, Dr. Maxwell Fitzpatrick. The doctor didn't hesitate, but said, "Osman Ratchet, sir, I am prepared to make you a rich man again. The pay is excellent, if you just work for me."

Osman turned to Akkikiktok. "How does San Francisco sound to you?"

"Yes, please," she responded in Inuit.

Osman gathered the notes for the Immortality Serum, vowing to get his hands on as much oxy-helium as possible. "We go together, then," he replied. "Always travel in pairs," he thought. "And never forget!"

The River Lethé flowed on, "the River of Forgetfulness."

CHAPTER TWELVE:
The Flooding of the Acheiron*

* "The River of Sorrow"

"Maxwell!" Osman Ratchet yelled to Dr. Fitzpatrick, "We've got a Code Grey on floor 36. An old woman is wielding her cane, which she sharpened with her finger-nails."

"Dr. Fitzpatrick hurried out of his private office and pressed the intercom. "Shawnka! Code Grey, floor 36, Sol Quadrant!"

Floor 36 of the Large Presidio Hospital Facility was in an uproar. Two nurses had already been stabbed through the heart. "It's the pimp," Shawnka sent back, "I'll handle it."

Shawnka's dark skin glistened with sweat as he rode the emergency elevator. The pimp was a special case of eideticism, or photographic memory, which the hospital collected. Especially dangerous, classified already as "an extreme danger to others."

The hospital chaplain, Chaplain Xao Lin, was intoning over the dead bodies, the bane of the hospital, as valuable research was lost. She was not sweating. "Dona nobis pacem." Grant us peace. "Pro libertate eos occubuisse." They died for liberty. "Indomitaeque morti!" Untamable death! "Durate et vosmet rebus servate secundis!" Carry on and preserve yourselves for better times! "Per aspera ad astra!" Through difficulties to the stars! she finally admitted tellingly.

Chaplain Xao Lin, the triple-agent, made a swift exit from the ward.

Shawnka rushed past, and with great alacrity put the pimp into a full nelson. She dropped her cane, yelled "Bitch!" and was hauled off to be strapped down in seclusion, with special electrodes to monitor functioning. But no official murder charges would be filed. Research was more important. This was a sign of the times, like the flooding of rivers. In the 40 floors of the Presidio Hospital, the patients were rebellious.

The National Security Council, working in conjunction with M5, British Secret Intelligence, had established the Presidio Hospital in San Francisco as a think tank. It studied counter-intelligence, remote viewing, memory and "unique" insight and increasing the I.Q., Psycho-motor Epilepsy and neuro-retinal feedback, hypnosis, neuro-linguistic programming, and designer drugs. It contained 4,000 patients but with a staff of only 102, hand-picked by other think tanks at Stanford and the University of California at Berkeley. Patients were only released through a special determination that they could be better studied outside rather than in. Few visitors were allowed, and no journalists. Reports were made weekly.

Dr. Maxwell Fitzpatrick was the Executive Director. He had been a professor of philosophy and linguistics at UC Berkeley. But his new assistant and Special Liaison, Osman Ratchet, was even smarter. His hawk-like eyes were sharp and penetrating. Except already the work was giving him grey hairs.

Their taster Diane brought them their meals. There were no obvious drug alerts from the cafeteria. Then Shawnka came to file his special report: "'Native' is hostile, physical, abusive, but not suffering dementia, in fact clear as a bell."

She had achieved a revenge for her incarceration. She would remain in seclusion for two years, one for each death. The hospital had time (or so they thought).

They lived in an era of suspicion. Their mission might be the difference between life and death for American society. The previous known photographic population had all been nuclear physicists, who could contain complex nuclear theorems in their heads. But Intelligence had acquired another 4,000 eidetic natives from all areas of the human population. They had become known only through a rigorous program of surveillance, lead by Hilda Bingen of Scotland Yard, the foremost known forensic psychic.

Dr. Fitzpatrick, as Executive Director, signed off on all of Shawnka's notes. Special Liaison Osman Ratchet the Third reviewed, and then they were sent to the Chaplain for her report, and she concurred.

"It was a bloody scene," Chaplain Xao Lin commented as she entered. "Cain slew Abel..."

"She must have wanted her isolation bad," Dr. Fitzpatrick enjoined. "I look forward to meeting one of her clients. Central Intelligence says three weeks, if they're lucky. Seems like this lady had a long career, though."

"She looks like Kali's grandmother," Osman commented, "and she's had hundreds of clients."

"They'll hand-pick one," Fitzpatrick returned. "It will be one of her prostitutes, not a john."

"Even Mary Magdalene was forgiven," the chaplain commented. "But we have failed in other respects so far. I recommend Kali here be kept on a life-long basis. She's not worth more on the Outside."

"I concur," replied the doctor. The expense to "the Company" would be less, too. Man-power was at a premium in this Age of Suspicion. Osman was turning back to his book, "Principles of Learning and Memory."

"Don't forget the twelve progress reports, Osman," chided the doctor.

"A bene placito." At ones pleasure, the chaplain overruled. "Ad astra per aspera." To the stars with difficulty.

"Sed quis custodiet ipsos custodes?" Dr. Fitzpatrick, the linguist, replied. Who watches the watchmen?

"Si vis pacem, para bellum," replied the chaplain. If you want peace, prepare for war.

"Stercus accidit," Osman interjected. Shit happens.

Osman read his book:

"If anything captures vividly the meaning of memory imagery it is the popular conception of photographic memory. We all dream of how life would be improved if we could scan the contents of a page - say, the conjugation of an irregular verb in a foreign language - and then effortlessly be able to call up any detail of that page later. This dream gives way to envy when we hear tales of people who actually possess such powers...

"Psychologists, however, have attempted to devise more easily standardized criteria for truly eidetic, or vivid, images.

"Woodworth (1938) advanced the 'schema with correction' hypothesis to cover instances where a form could be encoded as some deviation from a familiar object...

"The reproduced forms tended to be better figures, in the Gestalt sense of the term, than the originals..."

Osman Ratchet thought of his old friend Dr. Bell with deep regret. "Tempus fugit, non antem memoria." Time is fleeting, but not memory, he thought.

The chaplain was still there, watching him intently, even though a stare of more than 5 seconds was illegal, the lowest form of harassment.

"Venire facras." You must make come, she said.

"I prefer the Ogun language," Osman admitted.

"So do I," Shawnka interjected.

"But I'll find her, give me time. And pass me over those CIA photo line-up portfolios. I already have a sense of who she might be." He flipped through about one hundred of the natives clients. "That's the one," Osman revealed finally. "One Clea Berry. Last traced aboard a cruise from Fort Lauderdale to Atlantis Island. Premature white hair. Sensual. Affective, effusive, interested in cards. Bets high, enjoys tequila, reads People, the New York Times, and the Hollywood Gazette. Smokes Virginia Slims. Prefers chocolate. Family unknown. Awaiting further orders."

"Well?" queried the doctor.

"I'll need the chaplain with me," Osman stated for the record. He was watching her, too, although he had only suspicions.

"Arcana imperii." Secrets of the empire, she attempted to impose.

"It's between us four," said Shawnka, as the Chief of Security since the death of "Bill."

"All for the cause," Dr. Fitzpatrick enjoined. "Russia becomes more influential every day..."

"We're off to Atlantis!" Osman cried. He deposited a brief note to Akkikiktok, and then the chaplain and he boarded a waiting limo. They would be fully equipped by Central Intelligence.

"Atlantis Island" in the Bahamas, still owned by the Sheratons, had an Atlantean Quay for yachts, a dome with a Starbucks franchise, the famous Bridge Suite, and an expensive casino.

Osman Ratchet and Chaplain Xao Lin lounged by one of the pools, amidst a tropical garden with fig-palms and aloe plants. "Would she take the Bridge Suite, or do you think she's saving for the casino?" Osman asked the chaplain. He had acute insight, but not psychism.

"An unlisted room, behind an airlock. But she'll come out to the casino, at least for the bar..."

"I'll be reading the London Dispatch in the lobby. You take position at the bar, no matter how long it takes. These coca leaves will keep us alert." He produced the CIA gifts and wandered away.

"That bastard!" Xao Lin thought. She continued recording in her memory.

By then, Central Intelligence had already given plastic surgery to three volunteers to make them resemble Osman Ratchet.

The chaplain proceeded to the bar, and ordered a margarita with extra tequila. The tequila would put her in good standing with this Clea Berry, who was more suspect than ever. She quickly texted the Kremlin as to her whereabouts with this first isolation from Osman. "To the stars!" she thought. The Gestapo ruled the KGB. But her greater devotion was to the Tong, the Chinese Secret Service. But she had left her comfortable position at the hospital: now greater uncertainty ruled the day.

Daylight was ending. It was happy hour at the casino bar, and it was crowded with gamblers from many lands. She awaited with anticipation the arrival of Clea.

In the lobby, Osman skimmed the headlines of the London Dispatch. "Presidio Hospital Quarantined Again: NASA Denies Involvement." "M5 Denies Using Torture." "Platinum Reaches All-time High." He scanned down:

"Vatican City. Despite ongoing preservation efforts at the Sistine Chapel, Michelangelo's Finger of God has become unglued and no longer touches Adam."

Finally he came to what he most wanted: "Monte Carlo, Monaco. A mysterious Dr. Bell has broken the bank at Monte Carlo, defying odds of trillions to one. He told Reuter's yesterday, 'I plan to settle in San Francisco. I shall presently take up a posting with the San Francisco Chronicle's editorial section.'"

"Ahh, he's alive," Osman sighed. He decided to desert the chaplain, and let her explain to the Presidio Hospital ("And whomever else," he thought acutely).

"To the stars!" the chaplain repeated to herself, as she observed the unmistakeable white-haired young woman enter the casino bar. Xao Lin had reserved a seat next to herself. "Would you like to sit here?" she offered Clea.

"Thank you," came the reply in a languorous tongue. "I'll have four blue margeritas, bar-keep." She removed gold bullion from her suede purse, including a large tip.

"Coming right up, miss."

Clea turned to the chaplain and said, "Aspice, officio fungeris sine spe honoris amplioris." Face it, you're in a dead-end job.

All the chaplains senses were alerted, even more than usual. The two psychics faced each other. "Have we met?" Xao Lin inquired.

"Better to be on a honeymoon," Clea returned, although she was not presently seeking suitors.

"And what is it you do?" Xao Lin pried.

"My parents died of an unknown virus. My father was a banker and my mother a famous artisan. All their money is mine now." She was already finishing her first margarita.

Chaplain Lin fingered the syringe in its case in the pocket of her skirt. She knew they had found one. "Cribbage?" she decided to say.

"Never that. Only poker and black-jack."

"I see," the chaplain replied. "And where are you from?"

"From the Okefenokee Swamp. I was born on holiday. Breach birth, y'know. Horrible dictu." Horrible to tell.

"Opus Dei," commented the chaplain. The work of God. "You're for the hospital," she thought to herself. But she sensed then that even thinking was dangerous.

Clea polished off her second margarita. "I'm due for the hospital," she stated quite unexpectedly.

"It just so happens I'm the chaplain at one of the finest. You know the Presidio in SF. What do you need hospital for?"

"I suffer from Psycho-motor Epilepsy and neuro-retinal feedback," Clea replied smoothly.

"We can help, my dear." Chaplain Xao Lin observed Clea's petite nose and elvish ears. "She might be our last patient," she couldn't help but muse. "To the stars! Our silver ghosts."

Beyond Vulcan was mystery. But in the basement of the Presidio Hospital was another, shielded in lead from prying minds. But the chaplain knew.

Already Dr. Joseph Nicholas Bell was investigating, dressed in his latest prosthetics, transforming him into a fat, elderly lady in food-service vestments. "Elevator going down," the attendant said. But the cafeteria was in the basement, and he wanted the sub-basement, for verification. He inoculated the attendant with an ampule of proto-heroin he had scared up in the Tenderloin, and stepped neatly into the sub-basement. He was confronted by massive titanium cylinders and laboratory technicians scrambling about.

"Sorry," he said in his best female voice, "The attendant made an error." He hopped back on the elevator. "So that's it, by George," he thought to himself. "The hospital is being made into a space-craft." Already, under the new quarantine, the hospital was being wrapped in tarps of Kevlar and titanium sheet metal under the guise of a retro-fit.

Dr. Bell entered a Starbucks bathroom and stripped down to his other prosthetics, his alias as "Monsieur Proust," with trim features and an angular face. He disposed of the old prosthetics by tearing them to shreds and flushing them, then proceeded in his customized Silver Shadow Rolls-Royce limousine with the Monte Carlo flag on it. "Why is it," he thought, "that I must go back to the hospital," which he had made a daring escape from. He could not depend on prosthetics, because they would give him a complete physical examination. He had to turn himself in as a patient, and as a former escapee. Little did he suspect his old friend Osman worked now at the hospital as Special Liaison. It was Dr. Bell's hope to become part of the staff (and, incidentally, raid the Morphine and Valium). Despite the lack of freedom, and loss of money, the gambit was irresistible. He had to know where that hospital was flying to, and its ultimate mission.

"What are you seeing?" Dr. Fitzpatrick asked Clea.

"Snow, black and white spots, bending space, and 'movies' in the retina."

"Definitely Psycho-motor Epilepsy. I'll give you a heavy dosage of Keppra."

She took her private room on "C" ward, which contained muted pastel colors and a dim, perpetual lamp, and then Clea luxuriated in a hot bath. As a psychic, she was awaiting the arrival of her husband. She had outwitted the CIA, and the chaplain. Even Osman Ratchet did not suspect.

Dr. Bell descended to his Presidential Suite, with perique soaked in rum, and ruminated. But time is of the essence. First, he donned his finest maroon silk smoking jacket over a natty black linen three-piece, a grey wide-brimmed crushable hat, and then all of his most valuable jewelry, including rings of deepest blue sapphires, yellow diamonds, and platinum, and three women's watches made of pure rose gold and platinum hands, valued at $100,000USD each.

He then gathered up his dozen pens of invisible ink, and taped into the lining of his jacket the ink pouch. His writing would require a solution of iodine to be revealed.

He shaved his mustache, removed his colored contact lenses, and headed straight to the hospital in a limousine.

"I'm here to be re-hospitalized," he declared. Almost automatically he was surrounded by men in black with green berets.

"You're in excellent health," said Dr. Rosenthal. "I shall classify you as a regular diet, and place you on "C" ward. You may keep your belongings, but beware of thieves. I shall also, for one of your rings," she added, "give you full commissary privileges."

Dr. Bell discovered Clea wandering about in hospital skivvies. "Nice day, miss," he said, actually in acute distress.

"Not to worry. I know you. I have remote viewing."

"We're trapped," the doctor replied, pleading for more.

"We have each other for now. They will scheme, and we will scheme." The odds were unknown to them both, as they were entangled in the sophisticated web of intelligence, counter-intelligence, and hyper-intelligence.

"Strictly speaking," came the reply, "we cannot evaluate futuristic prophecy, since its truth depends on subsequent events." He felt his blood pressure rising. A nurse entered "C" ward and pointed a Walker Automatic at Clea.

"Your time has come!" she spat.

"Your gun won't work," Clea replied calmly.

There was a click, but no bullet fired. The nurse backed down in embarrassment. Clea turned to Dr. Bell. "I will leave you to your Sanctum Sanctorum. I must take my Valium and sleep. Dr. bell automatically gave her one of the pink gold ladies watches, then retired to his quarters which he shared with a red-skinned Peruvian, feeling himself greatly relieved.

"She's magic!" he beamed. There was new hope in Purgatory. Yet against what odds? Who would live and who would die?

Dr. Bell had already died, on the moon. His heart had stopped beating for over three minutes. He had awoke with severe nausea from radiation poisoning, but after several days had managed to escape Middletown and catch an unmanned transport saucer back to earth. He had splashed down in the Mediterranean off of Monaco. Apart from counting cards illegally, he knew the spin constants for the Wheel of Fortune, and his own finesse. They would have thrown him out before the bank was broken, but with the Wheel of Fortune it was against regulations.

Now he would immerse himself in his notes, in invisible ink.

Executive Director Dr. Maxwell Fitzpatrick was consulting privately with Chief Liaison Osman Ratchet. "We have Clea, she turned herself in. And guess what! Dr. Bell has returned!"

"I live here from now on," Osman declared, and retired to the doctors resting suite for some television.

"New collagen body rinse, special offer: for those seeking the ultimate in skin healing and hygiene, order now. Operators are standing by during the breaks in tonight's programming."

Shawnka entered, his dark skin glistening with perspiration. "The natives are revolting," he said. "Nine Code Grey's today."

In strode an excited Chaplain Xao Lin. "The Vatican has made it official: the Rapture is soon. They're acquiring more wealth even as we speak."

"So I read," said Osman. "After three days He was arisen."

"He's been undercover a long time," Shawnka jested. He was becoming fast friends with Osman. After all, it was invaluable to find people you could trust. They decided to play a duet on the piano.

"Ora et labora." Pray and work, the chaplain interrupted. "Pallida mors." Pale death. "Pater historiae." The father of history. "Per astera ad astra!" Through the thorns to the stars!

"Have another placebo," Osman remarked. The chaplain exited in a fury.

Osman turned to Shawnka. "De inimico non loquaris sed cogites!" Don't wish ill for your enemy; plan it.

Dr. Bell was scribbling furiously. "The lamb was slain and came to life again. The Beast was and was not and is about to ascend. Who is like the Great City? No one could number who came out from great persecution. Many visions are inauthentic, as we see preparations for Armageddon, as before we saw a talking snake. But by the way, snakes do talk, perhaps more than others." He interrupted himself. "I must see the chaplain."

But just then a great rumbling reverberated throughout the hospital, but it was not another San Francisco earthquake. Titanium cylinders were spewing hydrogen fires. A deep blast separated the hospital from its moorings. The Presidio Facility incinerated San Francisco for blocks, as the tremendous weight of its vast 40 floors lifted into the sky. Every car on the Golden Gate halted screechingly.

Osman and Shawnka just looked at each other and laughed, as the fog flew past their window, and they lifted into the sunlight. They sang "Over the Rainbow" to each other in ridiculous delight.

Dr. Bell, with his mastery of automatic diagnosis, confronted the psychic Chaplain Xao Lin. He said immediately: "A fronte praecipitium a tero lupi." A precipice in front, wolves behind (between the rock and the hard place).

"A posteriori!" she spat. Inductive reasoning, based on observation, as opposed to a priori.

He returned: "Magna res est vocis et silenti temperamentum." The great thing to know is when to speak and when to remain silent.

"Silence is golden!" she threatened. "And fraternization is illegal in this hospital."

"For one thing, this is no longer a hospital. And secondly, we were only flirting. I await my objectives."

"You're crazy," she said with undisguised venom. "You need your meds! And I'm telling Dr. Rosenthal. Perhaps you require a lobotomy!"

"I'm used to the howling of wolves. But your bark is worse than your bite. Far worse, I might add."

"There is strength in numbers," replied the triple-agent.

"I already used that line. Some things I can guess. Now comes the competition for limited resources, and I require a nurse for my prescribed Valium and nicotine gum. You, however, are an unsolvable mess."

The chaplain fumed away in disgust, to find someone to report to. But exiting the ward, she was blocked by Clea. There was just a moment's pause, and Clea punched two fingers with Shou Lin agility into the chaplain's kidneys, which burst. A series of strong thumb blows arrived then to the chaplain's pancreas. Then an expert pinch on the neck, and the chaplain was knocked out. She would never speak again, and there hadn't been time to cry out.

Clea faded into the meandering patients, whistling, and awaited lasagna for dinner. "Know when to speak..." she said to herself with delight.

Dr. Bell received this note from Dr. Fitzpatrick: "You shall post-haste be hired onto the Board of

Directors as Chief Psychiatrist, to revise any and all cases of ignoring regulations, or potential cases, and additionally to scrutinize hospital procedures and personnel. Sincerely, Dr. Maxwell Fitzpatrick. P.s.: Chief Liaison Osman Ratchet jovially welcomes you aboard."

"Sir Osman Ratchet!" Dr. Bell exclaimed. "He and I are on the same page! Use it or lose it," he jested.

The Presidio Hospital crashed through the satellite barrier on the plane of the ecliptic, and jaunted past the moon, videoed there by NASA specialists. The orbits of Venus and Mars quickly disappeared behind them, and the Saturn Luxury Accommodations flashed brilliantly for a few moments.

Uranus, Neptune, and Pluto faded from view, and Planet X came and went. Vulcan loomed larger and larger. The hospital finally passed the last man-made satellite, engines reversed propulsion, and they landed with a fleeting gentle moment on the planet Vulcan. The staff of the "Presidio" launch breathed with a temporary relief, and the inmates fumed. They were all robbed of earth, except for the limited supplies.

Dr. Bell, wearing a doctor's smock with badge over his maroon silk smoking jacket, made his first recommendation to the rest of the Board of Directors: "All patients and personnel below the 40th floor should be nullified, except Miss Clea Berry. This can best be accomplished by gaseous Chloroform through the air ducts, which shall anesthetize them until each individually may be destroyed in the appropriate manner after observation. Additionally, it is my recommendation the Board of Directors disband in favor of strict meditation. Personnel and patients on the 40th floor should then be joined by them for further observation. This letter is strictly confidential and private, except as I see fit."

The advantage to the rest of the Board of Directors was evident: more supplies to go around. They agreed unanimously, all eleven of them (whoever they were).

They hoped to continue living until an investigative team could land and rescue. Only one man knew the real answer: Dr. Maxwell Fitzpatrick, former Director-in-Chief of NASA.

Dr. Bell took Shawnka with him to observe the Chloroformed bodies one by one. Shawnka first showed him the body of the lady with the cane in seclusion. "She's hideous," he noted calmly. "Is she the worst in your experience?"

"I think so," answered Shawnka.

"Every one of our victims shall be burned alive, then," Dr. Bell ordered. "Begin dismantling the wooden chairs...and make the fire in the elevator shaft. To reduce electrical usage we'll use the stairwell."

"You know," spoke Clea softly and lightly to Dr. Bell, "You might not understand neuro-retinal feedback."

"What kind?" he asked sympathetically.

"Like speeded up movies, uncontrolled eideticisms of the retina."

"The eyes are part of the brain," he observed simply.

"It makes me sleepy," she commented, not to mention the Valium.

"You are feeling sleepy..." intoned Dr. Bell.

"I am feeling a little sleepy, now that I mention it," she joked.

"You can see your mothers face when you were an infant. She is singing you a lullaby..."

"Out of pitch," noted Clea.

"You've had your milk, room temperature. The L-tryptophan is taking effect..."

"By George, I think I've got it!" declared Clea. "Like the seashore..." She fell into a trance.

Dr. Fitzpatrick arrived. "Dr. Bell, I've come to show you this." He hauled in an inflatable bed. "These," he announced, "are from NASA."

"Yes..." Dr. Bell said.

"We also have a small rocket. It will take forever, but, properly coated, these beds can be attached to a tether. We can then fire the tethered rocket to earth and tow our way back on these beds..."

"I've got a better idea, let's tow ourselves to Saturn!" cried Dr. Bell. "Earth was never what it was, I prefer solitude and good company."

At that moment, the door was rapped on. "Who is it?" rasped Clea, deep in trance.

"We're the three survivors of the Vulcan 5 mission. We were texted we'd be rescued."

"Down the hall to your right," Clea intoned, "but we don't have enough hydrogen."

"NASA meant more people, not less. We live in a pyramid from some sort of other civilization. We were awaiting your arrival, so that you would stay."

"He speaks the truth," put in Dr. Fitzpatrick.

"Saturn can wait!" declared Dr. Bell.

"Not to worry," came the voice beyond the door.

"Good advice," Dr. Bell returned.

"We found these inscriptions," Corpsman Nathaniel Iff spoke excitedly. "The time-line, according to our Universal Decoder and our anthropologist Dr. Rosemary, begins at 26,000 b.c.e., but ends in a few weeks. We were eager to be here, after Vulcan 1 arrived."

"What happened to 2, 3, and 4?" Dr, Bell asked directly.

"Nobody knows," explained Dr. Fitzpatrick.

"I'm going to Saturn, with Clea," said Bell.

"Shawnka?" queried Dr. Fitzpatrick.

"I'll stay. Someone has to manage the inmates," replied Shawnka.

"Feed them through the slot," said Dr. Bell. He was used to giving commands. "And then check every two weeks to see if anyone can officially be categorized 'low risk.' Good luck!" cried Dr. Bell.

Clea and he had a long tow to Saturn, but closer shaves had happened. The Saturn Luxury Accommodations would be perfect. They lay strapped to separate inflatable beds, and towed along slowly to Saturn. Occasionally they stopped to play a game of "space cards" and drink Tang.

Osman Ratchet was reviewing the inscriptions closely. Every curve of the hieroglyphs, every apostrophe. After two weeks he became paranoid.

"Good-bye, Dr. Fitzpatrick. I'm towing myself to Saturn." His dark, hawk-like eyes over hawk-like nose sparkled with admonition.

"I must stay," said Dr. Fitzpatrick.

"I'm going with him," Shawnka included, gesturing to Osman. "You can feed the crop."

"Something performs experiments," Osman whispered to Shawnka.

"I've heard of that, too," Shawnka replied under his breath.

"These inscriptions aren't right. I don't think they can reach light speed. They may be around now."

"Let's hurry," Shawnka agreed.

The residents of the 40th floor were pounding on the steel door, as Osman and Shawnka floated off on tethered beds.

Dr. Fitzpatrick was peering into the view screen on board the wreck of the Vulcan 5. He had left the rest where they were. He observed an asteroid floating towards the planetoid.

"We are the People of the Asteroid," came a voice over the intercom. But Dr. Fitzpatrick tried to ignore it. The asteroid revealed no telemetry.

But then he saw it moving to the wreckage of the Presidio, where electronic arms dismantled the hull and vacuumed the inhabitants of the hospital on board, through an airlock that only looked like a crater on the asteroid. It then proceeded to the pyramid, and the survivors of the Vulcan 5 were likewise taken away.

Dr. Fitzpatrick quickly put on his helmet and began leaping over the plain in the light gravity. The asteroid checked the wreckage of the Vulcan 5. But Dr. Maxwell Fitzpatrick was back in the Presidio Hospital's Large Array. The asteroid went in the opposite direction. Maxwell watched through a portal of the hospital, frozen in place, breathless. Then he came to, and swiftly texted

Tululah at NASA Headquarters: "E.T. Vulcan is evidently not benign. Comes in shape of small asteroid. May not have warp propulsion. Notify Geneva immediately. Non-warp crafts are multi-generational. Strong hint of 'venal' class. Move headquarters from Pyrenees, and alert the Director of Central Intelligence. Inscriptions will arrive soon."

Immediate action would be taken.

CHAPTER THIRTEEN:
Living in the Styx*

* "The River of Hate"

The Saturn Luxury Accommodations were nearly deserted, after the disaster on the moon. The eminent Dr. Bell and his learned disciple Clea had received complimentary accommodations in the Royal Suite. Even Shawnka and Osman had received free rooms, and unlimited bar tabs. The Accommodation was attempting to gain free advertising.

Shawnka and Osman were playing a duet in a room just off the Rings Lounge on an antique Steinway piano. But Dr. Joseph Nicholas Bell and Clea Berry were in their chambers. He was again putting her under hypnosis.

"Watch the watch..." he intoned softly. Her blue-green eyes moved back and forth with the watch.

"I see the Holy Mountain. I am walking in a valley. I see olive trees, cypress, willow, oak, and the famous cedars..."

"There is a calamity..." answered Dr. Bell, a master hypnotist among other things.

"I see Strangers lurking in the heart of the woods...there are piercings and tattoos of skulls...but amidst them is one who comes from the very depths, the graven image of the Unholy One, his face like a laughing skull..."

"This man has a name..." Dr. Bell suggested to Clea.

"His name is Abaddon, the Angel of Death. He is preparing for war. He holds a dark onyx ball in his hand and looks within, searching. He preaches to his followers..."

"Where are they from, these people?"

"They are from the ark. They are the People of the Asteroid..." Clea began to look frightened. Dr. Bell decided to end the session.

"What is their purpose?" was his last question.

"Ask not for whom the bell tolls, it tolls for thee!" Clea intoned, a tear in her lovely eyes under sheet-white hair.

"When I snap my fingers you will awake. You will remember nothing."

"I will remember nothing."

"The inscriptions were all wrong," Osman said to Shawnka's friendly dark visage as they played backgammon. "The anthropologist from the Vulcan 5 got it wrong. I noticed a few accents that seemed to be archaic, referring to the Bringer of Doom, the death that haunts us all."

"Who would believe such a story as to make it their own?" asked Shawnka.

"Kali's grandmother would," Osman Ratchet commented. He lit a fine perique cigarette. "Do you think that someone might show?"

"The time-line is probably right," answered Shawnka, flexing his heavy shoulders.

Dr. Bell burst into the gaming room. "I don't think the laser array will work for us!" he declared. "When they arrive, I'm going onboard with a jet-pack." He paused, and then continued by way of explanation. "Always look Doom in the face. There's someone I have to meet." Clea entered drowsily, and the dolled-up hostess served complimentary margaritas and cinnamon liquor with gold flakes.

"We're with you all the way," Osman vowed.

"I can't take Shawnka or Clea. But I need you, Osman. Always travel in pairs..."

Osman's hawk-like dark eyes flashed as he put out his cigarette in a crystal ashtray with the insignia of the Accommodations, two lions rampant, one white and one red. "I fear a little." He sipped some liquor.

The doorbell from the magnetic security grid rang loudly, jarring everyone. "We're not answering it!" Dr. Bell insisted to the hostess.

The Universal Decoder came out over the intercom. It rasped and garbled for awhile, and then spilled out a hideous phlegmatic sound. "We are the Egeria Asteroid of Alpha Centauri. Prepare to be boarded."

Dr. Bell proclaimed: "The best defense is a good offense." To Shawnka and Clea he said, "Lock yourselves in the Royal Suite after ordering." To Osman he preached, "We go in the name of Our Lady!"

"Our Lady!" Osman agreed instantly.

Clea looked terribly nervous and upset. "Do not worry, dear," said Dr. Bell. "Hope can be wrestled from darkness."

He and Osman raced for the suits and jet-packs, downing margaritas.

"I'm almost ready," said Osman. On their way, they selected special armaments from the gallery. A porter was about to object, but then thought better of it.

"Prepare to be boarded," shouted Osman keenly into his radio. The duo shot in their jet-packs directly at a particular crater of the asteroid, which registered as a hologram. They arrived in an atrium of alien palm-fronds.

Clowns capered and danced, white and red in make-up. They wore piercings and tattoos of skulls. But directly in their midst came the prime player from stage right. His white skin was shrunk around his skull, and he bore the scarification of a Tibetan swastika on his brow. The others were clearly in terror, but continued their capering, only more slowly.

"I come as Malaclypse. You shall be for our menagerie."

"Take us there presently, O Malaclypse," Dr. Bell spoke harshly, with scorn. "Our weapons we bring as gifts. But let us keep our cigarettes." Osman was following every step of the way.

They were ushered swiftly into a glass bubble at the center of the asteroid. Within were many creatures, mainly animals that had been strangely cloned. But also the survivors of the wreck of the Vulcan 5 and the survivors of the 40th floor of the Presidio Hospital. Dr. Bell and Osman Ratchet were shoved inside with nothing but their skivvies and their cigarettes.

Dr. Bell waited for the capering to cease. Eventually only Malaclypse remained, watching with a grotesque lear and contemplating experiments. But first he must satisfy his curiosity.

Dr. Bell, a master of forensic science, swiftly emptied the two packs of cigarettes. Malaclypse had never seen one before. Although he was the oldest, he was still descendant of a distant generation on Alpha Centauri's M-class planet.

Dr. Bell proceeded to lick his fingers and apply saliva to the strip of glue binding the papers of the smokes and applied them in a circle on the inside of the bubble. From the last one he withdrew his old flint-stone, which he always carried (never be without fire). He ignited the special cigarettes, which were full of salt-petre, or gun powder. A red-hot flare completed the circle of the cigarettes, and Dr. Bell pushed the circle of glass outwards. He, despite his exceeding age, somersaulted through, and came to grips with "Malaclypse," their hands on each other's throats. Osman knew he could not help, it was the Synchronicity, age against age, and could not be touched. Destiny must be followed sometimes. He gestured the others in the menagerie to remain calm and quiet.

Malaclypse was draining the life-force from Dr. Bell as they grappled. But Dr. Bell had secret reserves. After all, he had survived the oranur radiation on the moon.

"Ten thousand typhoons!" he gasped as they strangled each other. "Why won't you die?"

"I do not need oxygen," Malaclypse croaked. "Utter your prayers!"

"To Our Lady!" yelled the doctor. With his thumb, he ripped out the evils jugular vein, and blue blood spurted through the air, splattering the window of the menagerie grotesquely. Malaclypse lost his grip, literally and figuratively.

"I hate you!" came his final words. "I shall see you on the Other Side, in the River of Fire!" he collapsed in a blue pool, glistening and turning even whiter.

Dr. Bell gestured to Osman, and Osman understood. He pushed the three surviving members of the Vulcan 5 through the portal, the ring of fire, and gestured for the hospital personnel and staff to remain. "Make friends on your new home!" he commanded them, his eyes flashing darkly with admonition.

One of the Board of Directors, Dr. Rosenthal, immediately objected. "We're going to the Saturn colony!" she demanded.

"You stay here, because you're insane!" Osman almost screamed. "We've had enough!" He somersaulted through the portal, and the five raced for the decontamination unit where more space-suits awaited. They took five for themselves and ejected the rest into space.

Later that evening, Clea and Shawnka were much consoled. Shawnka continued to play solitaire without questioning, and Clea was gazing into a crystal ball.

A small rocket tethered itself outside that night, and Dr. Maxwell Fitzpatrick came along on an inflatable bed. "All's well, I see. Unless I'm gravely mistaken, the asteroid is nullified."

"It will be back," Dr. Bell said presciently, by way of inductive reasoning. "But not for a while. The insane must confront the insane."

Dr. Fitzpatrick paused momentarily. "I'll text NASA. Time is of the essence. I'll stay here for awhile, though."

Dr. Bell replied, "Nil ego contulerim incundo sanus amico." While I am sane I shall compare nothing to the joy of a friend.

CHAPTER FOURTEEN:
The Weeping of the Kokytos*

* "The River of Lamentation"

Naphthali was weeping like a shedding terebinth tree. She sat outside the Cafe Trieste in North Beach, San Francisco. "All my friends are gone!" she bemoaned to herself. Her tears were heavy with salt.

An elderly gentleman wearing a maroon silk smoking jacket sat reading the San Francisco Chronicle next to her. He pretended with all his strength not to notice.

"What's your name?" she said, as though detecting a diffidence.

"Archimedes Jones," Dr. Bell lied. "Pleasure to make your acquaintance. And what is your name, my dear miss?"

"Naphthali. I've lost my best friends," she admitted immediately.

"You are a daughter of the universe," Dr. Bell replied, yet, he sensed, with no sympathy. He reached out empathically at this. "Your friends may reappear..."

"They were all at the Presidio Hospital. Even my friends in the Tenderloin have deserted me..."

"It is a sad tale, and perhaps long, but one that must be told..." he said leadingly. After all, he had only left

Saturn for this meeting. It had been a fine point of Holmesian deduction, but he was a master of forensics. There had to be one "Unknown" left in the City.

"I'll tell you everything!" Naphthali gushed, although somewhat coldly.

"Rachel is still sweeping," Dr. Bell replied, his empathic abilities increasing. He noted, of course, that this young miss wore all pink, with the flag of Switzerland as a button on her pink beret. "You are too young to be weeping so, except that life is long..." he added. She wore reflective ultra-violet protective goggles. But he was wearing black x-ray contacts. "At least she is radiating," he thought, hoping it was to himself. He perceived suspicious pinks and greens in her aura.

"Will you be my friend? My parents disowned me, and you look like a man of means..."

"I have here exactly one ounce of gold bullion," Dr. Bell replied, handing over a brick. He fleetingly grazed her hand, and sensed the heat. He left a small deposit of carbon paper on the brick.

"Cross my palm with silver?" Naphthali replied, ceasing her weeping.

"Just some Vatican coins," he was willing to admit. "You may contact me later through Schrumphf and Co., attorney's-at-law. But before I go, what is the real reason you're weeping so?"

"I'm weeping for myself," she admitted, frustrated. "I was going to live in the Presidio Hospital. I understand there was free Morphine and Valium."

"Ah," said Dr. Bell, fearing needles and unknown viruses suddenly. "Rachel will stop her sweeping. But never take a wooden nickel."

This last point seemed, most evidently, to infuriate Naphthali. But she said, "I'll look you up. A friend in need is a friend indeed."

"Everybody needs money. Next time you can give me the palm reading." "Cross my palms with silver, indeed," he thought privately, or so he hoped. This monster had to be stopped. "Well, I have to do the laundry and see my dentist and shampoo my hair and call my mother..."

This was an extra burn on Naphthali, and her radiation turned black with uncontrolled malice. He left her the newspaper. She tucked it into her pink plastic back-pack, and left for Currency Exchange. Her next mission was the Tenderloin, for some black market proto-heroin. She knew many fine chemists, at least. "Isis!" she invoked. She ignored the various shadow-teams observing her, cashed out into United States currency, and bussed uptown to the Tenderloin. And she would not forget the Vicodin.

"I think at last I'm doomed," Dr. Bell confided to his friends in Osman's luxury suite in the Old Chronicle Building. Osman, Shawnka, and especially Clea were all ears. "If I contract Auto-Immune Deficiency Syndrome from this young woman, give me the gel." Osman was tracking Naphthali's gold bullion by remote x-ray, which viewed the carbon paper attached to the brick. The trail lead finally back to the Cafe Trieste.

"She owns that cafe," he reported, "and is in league with Currency Exchange."

"She lied well," replied Dr. Bell. "She is a daughter of the universe, the Starchild." Most people would find the blonde, slim Naphthali quite attractive, but Dr. Bell was repulsed. "She weaves the webs of Ariadne..." he added. "The most tangled webs of the goddess. And in the guise of pink."

"That gentleman was fooled," Naphthali thought as she purchased from a reclusive chemist. "But frustrating..." she agreed to herself. "Something is wrong here."

She returned to the Trieste and her CIA contact, and handed him a photo she had taken by adjusting her glasses. "Most Wanted," she reported.

"Cigarette?" the man replied. "Peruvian blue flake." She never refused CIA cocaine. It was the most difficult drug to obtain. "You have done well." She removed herself to a nearby alley to smoke. "Who are his Ogunkhan?" she wondered. But Clea was in trance.

"She has established, and she comes in strength..."

"When you awake, you shall remember nothing." Dr. Bell snapped his fingers.

"Let me handle it," begged Shawnka.

"It's your baby," Dr. Bell said in relief.

"I'm not going out," Osman declared.

"I feel sleepy," said Clea.

Naphthali disinterred herself from the ladies room, and immediately admired Shawnka's muscular frame and gentle, jovial face. But he appeared deep in Hobb's "Relative Time."

"Cappuccino on the house?" she offered him.

"We are bound by water, as sure as water is bound by the moon," said Shawnka.

"Mere Ogum talk," she answered instantly. But plasma was transmitting telepathy to her poisoned brain, and she became doubtful of her statement. "What is your name?"

"Locke. But what's in a name?"

"Let me hear it, then," she insisted. Her luminosity terrified Shawnka, and her pink eyes, which insisted on the failure of love, the quixotic, the absence of life, and the wrath of a woman scorned. He would be careful, but he must obey. He spoke Ogun, not Ogum:

"Iba oooo ni ng o f'ojo oni ju ooo." It is with homage, homage profuse, that I intend to render all my chants today. "Abojsupo aramobiej'i." A man laden with forthcoming precipitation. "Okunrin gidigba n'igboo Jebu." You are the stalwart assailant confronting the enemy in Ijebu woodland. "Omo Itandogun." A person charged with firing a gun twenty times. "Ogun ni ng o sin, ng o s'n Eegun." I will always worship Ogun, I will never worship Eegun. "Ogun palarina sita gbangba." Finally, Ogun killed the go-between in the courtyard of the compound. 'Eni ina n bi ri tire loto." Whoever does not like this should set up his own Ogun. "Iba l'a o f'oni ju, are Ogun dolao." We shall devote all our chants today to homage paying. "Agbara-ojo l'Ogun." Ogun is a torrent of rainwater. "Kiniun igbo kijikiji." Lion of the thick forest. "Ike Ogun." The death of war. "Oran naa jo bi erin lojun mi." In my view. the occasion is one for laughter.

Naphthali laughed with excess. She had appeared to genuinely enjoy. But now she must destroy him. But Shawnka had his Auto-Immune Deficiency Syndrome prepared by Dr. Bell. A lightning swift move by the former Code Grey respondent was enough.

"Bastard!" she screamed, waking up the entire cafe. CIA security alerts flashed from vehicles all over the City.

"See how long you can survive on gel," Shawnka answered. He strolled boldly out, with confidence, and stepped neatly into a Silver Shadow stretch with the flag of Monaco on the hood. "Well done!" his driver Clea reported. "You can relax. Have a menthol light," she suggested.

But Shawnka was to die of a mysterious kidney ailment.

"I will never forget," lamented Dr. Bell. They shot Shawnka's body into the cold of outer space, in a sealed casket, for later cryogenic defrosting.

CHAPTER FIFTEEN:
The Stinging of the Phlegethon*

* "The River of Fire"

Dr. Joseph Nicholas Bell, Osman Ratchet, and Clea Berry were preparing to depart from the River Lethé, in the Valley of Ten Thousand Smokes in Alaska.

But they had no place to go except San Francisco for a final analysis, and then depart from there. It was inevitable, as heroes were few, and it was concomitant upon them. But they knew their very lives were in jeopardy, in any event.

This time, they checked into the Fisherman's Wharf Mandarin Hotel. Their first trip was to the Ripley's Believe It Or Not exhibit.

They were on high alert, with radio units in their ears. They knew evil was afoot, but they could not deduce what kind, neither by inductive reasoning, nor by psychism, nor by trance. But Clea had possession of remote viewing, so they knew where to go. Alcatraz Islands glass pyramids and four Egyptian obelisks shone in the bay.

The City itself was not looking well. The Plague, the Black Death (which had never gone away), had broken out in the Tenderloin. Leprosy had reared its ugly head as well, transported from the ghetto of Jakarta. The murder rate had never been higher. And the undercover agents had only increased.

"Why do I have this funny feeling?" Dr. Bell complained. "Our lives are in danger..."

"I concur," concluded Clea. Little did they know that plastic surgery had created three other versions of Osman Ratchet, who all wandered the City, working for the KGB (who happened to be the newly-formed 5th Reich).

"Should we visit the Canadian Consulate?" suggested Osman. "Ottawa is beautiful this time of year." It was a blazing Indian Summer. The heat was nearly unbearable.

"First to Alcatraz!" Clea proclaimed. They mutually agreed, and hopped aboard a ferry for the grand tour of antiquities.

The People of the Asteroid had landed, and Dr. Rosenthal, formerly of the Board of Directors at the Presidio Hospital, had reported to her only superior, Rufus ("red") Voynich. Voynich was waiting on the Rock.

The three stalwart compatriots observed the grandeur of Alcatraz: Velasquez, El Greco, Redon, Van Gogh, and the Egyptological exhibit. In one corner they came across another Osman Ratchet. "Do I know you?" the real Osman inquired.

"We were separated at birth," came the lie. "It is with great pleasure that we finally meet..."

"I haven't got the time of day," Osman replied. He already knew he was on the "most wanted" list. At least this fool might be mistaken for him, he thought. In any event, the KGB were not their interest.

"Starry Night" hung, with paint cracking from lack of preservation, in the main rotunda, where Voynich the Red sat reading a guide-book. He casually opened a vial, which emitted malarial mosquitos. He had already taken the antidote.

"A being from the asteroid," Clea noted presciently. "This is the beginning of the end." The Gestapo agents about were on "stand down" status, although they greatly desired "first contact."

Osman took a chair next to the "Red," and, in nervous anticipation, leafed through an old copy of the Strand magazine. Clea took her place at the bar for a margarita.

Dr. Bell lit his pipe illegally, the tobacco smoke drifting away in silent plumes. "Silence is golden," he thought, "but silence gives consent."

He approached Voynich, who had a fringe of beard over mottled skin, and was wearing all black with a monocle and gold signet ring.

"Haven't we met before?" queried Dr. Bell in a foreign accent.

"You are Dr. Bell, I know that well," came the response. Dr. Rosenthal approached, furious.

"Betrayer!" she fumed.

"Merely God's humble servant," came Dr. Bell's cool reply. "What's good enough for the gander is good enough for the goose. This person from the asteroid appears to be threatening me. Now, are you going to start? Morituri te salutamis." We who are about to die salute you. It was an appropriate ruse.

"You realize, doctor," said Voynich, "I'm taking you to Hell."

Dr. Bell turned on the heels of his black leather walking shoes, and gestured to Osman and Clea. "A swift depart," he advised. "This is a ghost, and he knows what he is saying."

"No!" sobbed Clea. "How will you return?"

"Beyond death lies the Great Unknown," Osman consoled.

Voynich smiled mirthlessly as the trio left. Revenge would be his. Revenge is potent, awesome, and unforgiving.

The friends locked the door to their suite at the Mandarin.

"Tempis fugit," time is fleeting, cried Clea.

"I shall return by July," Dr. Bell stated. "Abyssus abyssum invocat," Hell calls Hell. "The matter is elementary. They are irresistible, and, therefore, must be stopped."

The asteroid hung over the Golden Gate bridge, causing wide-spread panic and consternation.

Dr. Bell stood still and watched, actually enjoying the fog.

"Houston, we have a problem," Dr. Maxwell Fitzpatrick was informed.

Dr. Bell unfolded his cross-bow and fired a tethered arrow towards the asteroid, and with the press of a button began to be reeled up. "Sayonara," he saluted the crowd below.

Dr. Bell endured the People of the Asteroid from Alpha Centauri, and the former denizens of the 40th floor of the Presidio Hospital. He was observing what looked like a malformed okapi.

"How does this thing operate?" He had been onboard with the criminally insane for months, barely being fed bread and water.

Voynich the Red appeared. "Only I do that." Voynich handed Dr. Bell a loaded pistol. "Thirty paces," he commanded. It was a fair cop. Dr. Bell walked in a steady manner to be agreeable. Their backs were turned to one another. At thirty paces each, they turned and fired. But their bullets collided in mid-air.

Fortunately, Dr. Bell had secretly inserted a scattering pellet he had as a fake molar, which he had brought as a contingency measure. The pieces penetrated all over Voynich's mottled visage. The asteroid would hang above the Golden Gate indefinitely. But there was much applause from the assembled throng, who had been liberated from their Mephistopheles.

Dr. Fitzpatrick burst in through a hologramic crater. "You're coming with me!" he exclaimed to the weak and dazed Dr. Bell. "You work for NASA now. We will await 'second contact.' And by the way, work well done!"

"Elementary, my dear Maxwell," Dr. Bell returned. "But first, to Las Vegas. I need to earn more money for supplies."

Clea and Osman met Dr. Bell at the airport with many congratulations. "I understand the Aladdin Hotel and Casino is pleasant," he commented, "and pass me that whisky, Osman."

"Evil is not greater than good," Osman replied, "but it was by a hair."

Dr. Bell stated, for the record: "Ad eundum quo nemo ante iit." To boldly go where no man has gone before.

"Ad infinitum," to infinity, Osman replied. But before their silent meditation, calling up new answers, Clea interjected:

"Pavesco, pavesco." I'm shaking, I'm shaking.

Their humor would be returning. But from the Aladdin there was no return. Home at last, where the bluebirds fly. NASA would be pervasive for awhile.

On the flight, Clea was much relieved. She wrote in her journal:

"When you do a jig,
Then you're thinking big!
As long as you are harmless you are swell!
And if life hands you a candy,
Accept it, fine and dandy,
Chew it very slowly for the spell!
And if the heavens start to crumble,
Speak up! Let's not hear a mumble,
For we all need more provisions 'gainst our Hell!
Your voice may it be heard,
Like the singing of some bird,
For only you know the secrets you can tell!
Try against the fate,
Arrive early, not too late,
And throw a coin into the magic wishing well!
Life ends soon or later,
Be a lover not a hater,
'For you hear the tolling of that bell!

Jeremy Balfour

When your time runs out,
Give a skip and not a shout,
Never give your soul up to the sell!
When the truth is reckoned,
Come forward, as you're beckoned,
Don't go hide away inside your shell!"

CHAPTER SIXTEEN:
The Tempest of Euroclydon*

*A hurricane that struck the Greek Isles

Everything in the Aladdin Hotel and Casino in Las Vegas was bustling. Clea was at a bar with a margarita. Dr. Bell was winning, as usual, at the Wheel of Fortune, with his calculations of spin ratios and finesse. Former Chief Liaison Osman Ratchet was in the Library of Agrabah, sifting through the recovery of Persepolis and Shushan and Shouster, saved from the flooding of the Abzal and Kirah. NASA agents stood out everywhere. Dr. Bell had been hired as a Chief Analyst and Inspector. The three heroes not only had security clearance but classified identification papers.

Osman poured through for Aladdin, his favorite hero, but found nothing, only the hint of a magic flying carpet. He went to visit Dr. Bell.

Dr. Bell immediately said, "If they can do it we can do it. If we can just invent replicators, we can do it. Transverse and longitudinal wave-forms, should be simple. Then we retro-fit this casino like the Presidio Hospital, as a space-craft. We'll be safer on Saturn."

"Good idea. I concur," Osman agreed. They both noticed Clea becoming upset at the bar.

"I'll give her Morphine, and she'll go to bed..." Dr. Bell granted. "Hypnosis hasn't really been working lately." Their tremendous fortune supplied them with many things, and what they didn't get themselves they could always ask NASA for. "It'll take some time, but at last we'll be away from the KGB, and those other fellows."

Osman Ratchet was wearing a brooch at his collar that was glowing purple-blue.

"You certainly are intimidating with that brooch," Dr. Bell commented to Osman's hawk-like features.

"Imperiousness is the best revenge," Osman answered. "What has Clea been saying, lately, though?"

"She peered into her crystal ball and told me Las Vegas was becoming too violent, and the whole world unsafe now. The way I see it, the Aladdin would make a perfect addition to the Saturn Luxury Accommodations. A few months and we'll be there, at most."

"Then she can relax."

"We'll have supplies to spread out, and call it Agrabah. Libraries, temples, tea-gardens, gates and fountains..."

"It can be assembled." Osman immediately left to go to their Royal Suite and order online, after first texting Dr. Fitzpatrick, who was with NASA in Houston. By the end, NASA had converted every room in the hotel as the trio's private suites. All agents left. The basement was full of massive titanium cylinders for hydrogen fires. Saturn was near at hand.

Clea awoke from a fitful sleep of lucid dreaming. They had landed. The dread of space-flight began to leave her. She began to happily roam about, seeking out libraries and viewing treasures. Dr. Fitzpatrick was the only one to join them, for "second contact."

Saturn would never be the same. The sting of the Phlegethon was ended, but earth was consumed by geopolitical conspiracies. Yet our heroes would have none of this now.

Clea said: "Ad vitam paramus!" We are preparing for life! "Ad vitam aeternum!" For all time!

"The replicators are working. We'll have hologramic food. And the Immortality Serum is coming along. We'll produce much oxy-helium." Dr. Bell responded. "Bella gerant alii." Let others wage war, said Dr. Bell.

"Da mini sis cerevisiam dintam!" I'll have a light beer! said Clea.

Later, Clea wrote in her journal: "I spied Dr. Fitzpatrick at the bar with a very tall fair-haired gentleman. 'Second Contact' has been made. Alpha Centauri has evidently been able to track their asteroid for the criminally insane. The counter-intelligence on earth is finally reaching the event horizon. Distrust has reached the breaking point. But Nature shall have its way: earth shall be destroyed by a tempest. There is little anybody can do, except cloud-seeding. But we await further emissaries from Alpha Centauri, although we are not considering further voyage ourselves. We are content to remain forever in Agrabah. By telescope, however, we shall observe earth, and eventually it shall be colonized by Alpha Centauri, while human survivors shall be few. I am continually hoping that all is well with my beloved Dr. Bell and Osman, who have worked so diligently for the future, while I merely peer into it. In the meantime, in remembrance of Shawnka, I am learning Ogun:

"'Yo di on ap sonde chwal mwen.' They are testing my point. 'Tout nanchon genyen defo pa-yo.' All peoples have their flaws. 'Mwen di ye, rele l'a ye.' I say it is, cry out it will be. 'Que cavaleiro e aquela, que vem cavalgando pelo cen azal, que vem defender o cruzeiro do espaco.' That gentleman is the one, who comes riding through the blue sky, who is defender of the Southern Cross. 'Abo o mo'hun ti n be?' Are you not aware of what is happening? 'Iba nle n too maa io. Looo to niku ja wa lododo awa lo.' I salute you before I proceed. Indeed, death deprived us of our flower. 'Mo kile oo.' I salute the house. 'Ode n bo legbee. Ki i se pode o legbe.' Hunter, I thought you had egbe magic. It is true you have. 'Omi atan ni won n mu?' Who now drinks of heavenly water? 'E ma biinu onoo 'Roko.' Be consoled, offspring of 'Roko. 'Anaiya pata bi ona.' The courageous one is like the road. Peace be with you, Clea Berry."

The man from Alpha Centauri apologized to Dr. Fitzpatrick. "We caused you much trouble. The criminal masterminds from our planet outwitted us."

"I know. We nearly had the same problem."

"I am rightfully glad your special manpower had the ability to deal with them."

Dr. Bell joined them. "My pleasure, your honor..." he ingratiated himself without pretense.

"Please, no honors. We're desperately tardy."

Osman approached: "Dear new friend, do not be discomfited. In the midst of tragedy there are small lights that shine. Although Clea says clouds will blot out the sun and stars."

The fair-haired gentleman replied: 'Happens all the time. Industrial societies progress faster scientifically than they can catch up to scientifically."

"You're welcome to stay," offered Dr. Fitzpatrick.

Dr. Bell interjected: "Only for a time. The four of us require our solitude together, four is the stable number...and a good game of Bridge."

Clea joined them presciently with a card deck. "Tarot reading, anyone?"

The tall man from Alpha Centauri replied, "I'll take magic wherever I can find it..."

They all agreed.

After many rains, the fleet from Alpha Centauri arrived. The polluted earth had flooded, and the roads and buildings were weathering away. If civilization ends for no other reason, it is due to weathering. The underground bunkers had long ago run out of food.

But on their way, the Centaurian's had discovered Shawnka in his casket, frozen in space. They put him in a cryogenic de-freezing unit and gave him two cloned kidneys to solve his fatal ailment.

"Pleased to meet you," was his very first saying. "We are on the brink of a new era! Let those who sleep, awake!"

The tempest had ended earth, but had ended, itself. All darkness, all, leads back to the light, as sure as suffering is a crucible.

"My dear new friends," Shawnka continued, "there are many happy days ahead." He would be their new teacher. "I can show you how to find happiness."

CHAPTER SEVENTEEN:
The Disaster Aboard "The Argonaut"

"Ye gods! annihilate but space and time, And
make lovers happy."
- Pope, "Martinus Scriblerus...or The Art of
Sinking in Poetry"

"The Rogue" drifted, floated, weightless,
approximate to the center of the Milky Way, near
Cygnus X1. Time spread out before the crew in all
directions, a banquet that could not be touched. All radio
transmissions were ignored. And some of the five
members of the crew thought this was a good thing:
better to die in space, than to face the Unknown. Yet
destiny had other plans for The Rogue, which would not
escape observance forever.

Earth was long since past in space and time.
Nobody onboard The Rogue knew Earths fate, or even
its exact location. They felt utterly lost. They had run out
of hydrogen precisely when NASA said they would, yet
transmissions to home would be lost in the static of the
inter-stellar voids. It was a one-way journey, as they
knew it would be, or thought they knew. They were left
high and dry, waiting to be discovered.

Their replicators produced hologramic food from
transverse and longitudinal wave-forms. This, too, was a

limited commodity, as all energy supplies were doomed to run out. The only thing unlimited was the space-time surrounding them.

Alexandro Patel was the captain, Arthur Wright the first-mate. The Highly trained crew consisted of Marie Foster, Sophia Price, and Alice Baker. Of the five, none of them desired, despite their predicament, to see home again. To them, earth was a dead place, the stars only were alive. But the stars also contained dread. They awaited either the shining glory of a new day, or the otherwise inevitable descent into the underworld, a world of infinite negative possibilities, or perhaps the ultimate fate. Their one-way voyage would be a voyage either into Heaven, or into Hell. For the time being, they considered themselves among the damned, unless for a requiem, as though they were caught in Purgatory. They could not anticipate the Judgement of Purgatory.

Their bone density was steadily decreasing due to outer space, and their replicator rations were running low. All had a feeling of space sickness. It was the captain, Alexandro Patel, who was the first to reveal signs of psychological unsteadiness.

"Who," he asked the assembled crew, "will be the first to taste Paradise, and immortality?" The rest hesitated.

"We shall begin to know," Arthur Wright, the first mate, put in hesitantly. The crew did not wish to alarm the captain.

"Our journey has just begun..." enjoined Sophia Price. Marie Foster and Alice Baker looked to her hopefully, that she would say more. "We shall not taste of death," she added, "only destiny."

"We await the coming of the Holy Ones," replied Captain Alexandro Patel. "Now that we have reached galactic center, destiny awaits." But they would have a long time waiting. Months, in earth time, went by, and their replicator rations were running low. The captain was increasingly unsteady. "Soon..." he intoned. "Destiny demands an answer..." They felt pangs of hunger as they rationed their dwindling supplies.

"There is no movement to be seen," commented Arthur Wright. But he didn't want to contradict the captain. "Yet, the moment must be soon..."

Marie Foster was the first to feel like she might be dying. No amount of medication would cure her lingering space sickness. "It must be soon," she said. Alice Baker held Marie's sweaty palms.

"I saw an elephant in my dreams," said Captain Patel, "and it said to me: 'only be afraid of mice.' We have nothing to fear but fear itself. Unless we fear ourselves..."

"Are we mice or men?" Arthur replied mildly. "Let's replicate some cheese, and like mice in a maze, find our way to our true destination."

Perhaps there's no such thing," Sophia Price said. But then she thought her statement unwise.

Arthur corrected her. "No, there is cheese."

"The moon is made of blue cheese," said Marie Foster hungrily. They were eating like mice. She passed away into Oblivion. The rest of the crew saluted as her casket was propelled briefly into outer space.

"We await the Day," Captain Alexandro Patel continued, unabated. "She is of the walking dead." She had been cryogenically preserved, just in case, but it had used up expensive energy reserves. And it made them all think of death. Even the captain began feeling uncomfortable doubts. "We live in uncertain times," he said airily.

First mate Arthur Wright's duty was to comfort the captain. "She merely passes away into the Great Beyond," he spoke, "from which there is every hope of return..."

Sophia Price was the next to die. She was cryogenically preserved, but to save energy was not propelled into space, but kept onboard. The captain again waxed philosophic. "We live in uncertain times," he repeated, as though by rote. "Yet, things will improve once we get back to earth."

The other two remaining crew members looked at him askance, knowing, or thinking they knew, that a return to earth was a lost cause. They all fell to writing in their respective journals, avoiding the eyes of the other two. CygnusX1 barely shone outside. It was almost perpetual night, as the sky expanded away from them. Their atomic clock ceased functioning. They were Somewhere in time.

"The Holy Ones shall find us soon," Captain Alexandro Patel wrote, "and again we shall know Food. And we shall be acclaimed, as survivors of a distant star. Our destiny awaits, triumphant, written. The only concern is the first mate, who has been acting strangely lately."

Arthur Wright put pen to paper: "The galaxy is as yet as mysterious as the runes on Excalibur. If only the Lady of the Lake would reveal her mysteries. But she comes with the sirens of the Deep. My Chinese is failing me. I must eat. But we are giving Alice Baker double portions, as she is growing thin."

Alice Baker was not yet anorexically thin. But she felt a certain "thinness." "Failure is not an option," she wrote. "At least the food is good. I must keep my spirits up." So she wrote her quixotic poetry:

"The witch said to her familiar cat,
'Surely, you are not up to all that,
To be more powerful than a toadstool,
More attuned than a bat,
Cooler than the coolest pool,
More constant than a hat,
More useful than a common tool.
Now you must go back to school,
Though you don't know where it's at:
I can tell by the way you've sat.'
And said the cat,
'In a word, you think that I am fat,
But I am just relaxing, and I purr,
After eating fondue from a vat,
Which is very taxing, I assure.
But let me tell you now,
As your familiar, except the sow,
I know you, but you know me no-how.
You've got it backwards,
Like the moon jumped over the cow.'"

Soon the meal-bell would sound. Alice could almost taste the food. But before this could happen, the infra-red telescope alarm sounded: an unidentified object was rapidly approaching from deep space.

"At last, the butler," Captain Patel exclaimed.

"We might serve them," the First Mate Arthur Wright pointed out, hoping for a sane response. "Let's put on our space-suits, just in case."

And he was right. The approaching object was a meteor, which slammed noiselessly into The Rogue, crushing open part of the titanium hull. The three survivors were ejected into the vacuum of space in their suits, emblazoned with the pyramid from the dollar bill. "Novus Ordo Seclorum," a new order shall be founded. They hadn't enough time to tether themselves together, and floated apart from each other. Only Alice was barely able to grasp a sheaf of The Rogue's torn hull, and climb back into the wreckage. Captain Alexandro Patel radioed Arthur Wright: "Houston, we have a problem," he jested merrily, "our flotation devices have come unstuffed!"

"Man your station," the first mate replied, "and use your propulsion unit, if you're facing in The Rogue's direction." A flare went off from the captains suit, but he was propelled in the opposite direction from the craft.

"Blue moon, blue moon," Arthur heard him singing as he drifted away from the center of the galaxy towards CygnusX1. Arthur Wright made it safely back to The Rogue, where Alice Baker was sealing the vent with plastic tarp. They then unsealed the extra oxygen, released the heating reserves, and removed their helmets.

"It's never been so good to see anyone before," Arthur commented.

"You look terrible," came Alice's reply, "have a wash and a shave. I'll spare you my water."

"Not in the slightest," Arthur said.

Sophia Price's cryogenically preserved dark eyes stared at them blankly.

"Perhaps the captain will make it to one of the planets," Arthur said hopefully. But they had detected no life there. The two sat down to a dejected game of chess, although they both felt lucky to be alive. The only positive point was that now the food rations would last longer.

"The Blood of Christ is spilt, even as we drink from the Cup," wrote Arthur later. "The Holy Grail of astronomy is null and void. There is no life in our neighborhood, only darkness. But, at least, we know we are near some M-class planets. The wine might be replaced in the Cup, as if by some kindly chaplain. We now have only two weeks of replicator energy left. We have decided to replicate champagne." They toasted life, they toasted even fate, and they toasted each other. They shot another round of flares like fireworks, hoping against hope.

Alice Baker wrote in her journal:
"My cuckoo clock sits upon my wall,
When it chimes, the cuckoo comes to the call,
And sings as many times as true,
Or I take the clock back,
But the shop has closed, alack!
Time is the most uncertain thing of life,
It runs out be life good, or strife,
But the cuckoo is made of wood, knows nothing of this,
It only calls because time is,
As it only should, and it feeds my soul,
To know time goes on, I yet have a goal,
Be it as uncertain as a wooden clock,
Whose cuckoo has begun to mock,

And if I could, I would wake my cuckoo to know it
is good,
And not know fate
(That there, in life, is too little, too late).
I say to my cuckoo, awake!
For the time is running late.
If she was alive, like a parrot,
She would say, 'You go to the garrote,'
For tempting fate without the means,
To live forever, as in our dreams.
So time ticks by, then chimes,
And we are done in, with no better signs,
Then to say fate rules, every time.
Time is fate, and I believe I am late,
For a very important date:
My last breath, which I abhor,
Knowing nothing lies behind the door.
Mortality is mans most major trait,
Which always arrives to end the score,
Though if wound properly, the cuckoo keeps on
singing.
Let your life be long, with clocks a-ringing,
With every moment as though your last,
For you cannot change the past,
But must live, for such time as be,
Though the wooden clock destroyed the tree,
Live for the future, don't look back,
Though the parrot mocks,
Tells you to work, and clean your socks,
And gradually, you come to hate the clocks.
Find yourself a ship, and mind the tack,
Don't look over your shoulder,

Unless time has no lack."

The Rogue was about to be discovered. A long sleek ebony ship like a submarine was skimming past noiselessly. The sensor array aboard The Rogue was still intact. There came a chime like a cuckoo clock. The Judgement of Purgatory was about to end.

First Mate Arthur Wright broadcast welcomes in twelve languages. After what seemed like an eternity, a voice radioed them back, hoarse and rasping through the universal translator: "We have detected your heat signatures...we see that you are marooned...we do not have a decontamination unit for unknown viruses, but will have a sister-ship rendezvous with you in two weeks time. Meanwhile, we will eject in your direction a cache of water and extra fuel cells. Expect "The Mermaid" in two weeks..."

The pair hugged each other in relief, and then fell to wondering about their fate. Expect the unexpected, they told themselves. For who were they bound to meet? The Rogue would be saved by The Mermaid. But would The Mermaid be saved by The Rogue?

After their last, final two weeks of replicator rations, The Mermaid began to salvage The Rogue. Arthur and Alice peered into the view-scope on the starboard side, as giant magnets lured their metal craft into a geodesic sphere, silver, hanging in space mysteriously. It bore the single sign of an isosceles triangle in gold. Arthur and Alice docked into a decontamination unit and were sprayed with foreign botanical extracts, and their ship was doused in hydrochloric acid. No one was on board The Mermaid except a single android, with pale skin and wearing red stripes. He also wore a badge that read "Decontamination Unit 95," but to Arthur Wright and Alice Baker, the hieroglyphs were meaningless, although they resembled Arabic script.

A recorded message said over a loud speaker, "You shall be taken to "The Bounty" for indoctrination and citizenship procedures. We welcome you in the good faith of future friendship. You may now don your oxygen masks." This the pair could understand through the universal translator. All things appeared perfectly acceptable.

The android said briefly, "Welcome in the name of peace."

"Are questions allowed?" asked Alice wisely.

"Only answers are allowed," the android retrieved from his comedy programming gel-pack.

This seemed reasonable. "Where are we going?" queried Arthur.

"The planet was overcome by a deluge, and we have no moons, so we live in space aboard our cars. We possess major space factories which produce spacecraft of various sorts for the population. You will be taken to a Dormfa Royal Suite Hotel, aboard The Bounty, that is floating nearby below sensors. I hope you enjoy a good casino," said the android.

The pair chuckled to each other for their incredible good luck. Arthur was contemplating the Grail, as Alice was writing rhyme in her head. They docked with the orange-red Bounty after a few hours, and were led to a lounge suite of whites and reds. The indoctrination recording enunciated, "You will find relaxing communal areas open 32 hours a day, on the port side. Minimum bid per hand 5 credits, maximum bid per hand 10,000 credits..." Arthur Wright and Alice Baker nearly laughed out loud.

In the casino, they discovered, sitting at a booth, Captain Alexandro Patel, quite drunk on blue raspberry margaritas. "My dear old friends, we meet again. As lucky as the number seven,"

he practically sang. "Try the root beer, it's out of this world..."

"And so we meet again," Arthur replied. "Your optimism has been rewarded. However improbably, Arthur thought to himself. In a corner of the casino lounge he noticed the frozen body of Marie Foster, which was bound for more complete freezing. Other guests mingled among the gaming tables, all looking basically human, except for some taller people. Recorded muzak played in the background. But Alice noticed something out of the ordinary: There were no older people present.

"Where are all the senior citizens?" she asked the captain.

"All frozen, you see. Once you've used up all your gaming credits, they put you into the deep freeze. Wonderful culture," the captain commented. Arthur and Alice had each been given 5,000 credits. The captain had already spent some of his on the Wheel of Fortune. "The more you lose, the younger you'll be when you wake up again. Wonderful culture," he repeated.

Alice shivered from the mere thought. But she wanted desperately to win at cards. "This is a fool's paradise. And where are all the children?"

"They're not allowed in casinos until they're twenty, when they're granted their credits. Wonderful system, keeps everybody happy. A preserved youth, an enjoyable pastime, then the chance at immortality while still young. It was voted in by all the computers..."

"I'm spending my credits on root beer," Alice commented hungrily.

"Your credits will never last," said the captain. "It's worth risking a game now and then, just to test the waters, so to speak, see if luck is on your side. I met one man who was fifty, he was so lucky with the slot machines!"

"This isn't quite right," Arthur whispered under his breath to Alice. And android offered him a drink.

"That will be five credits, please," it chimed like a cuckoo clock. "Have a nice day."

"This is good root beer, though," commented Arthur.

"But you are one step closer to death," whispered Alice. "What if you're never unfrozen?"

"I see your point. The root beer isn't that good."

"The game of life is the game of death," said Alice.

"It's only life," interjected the captain. "If you want me, I'll be at the baccarat tables..."

"This place is less sane than the captain," remarked Alice. She and Arthur returned to their deceptively luxurious

apartments, and there decided to play watch and wait. The casino seemed to be run by androids, who were directed by a central computer. "We must escape before our credits run out. Let's avoid room service." But they did put some coins into the slot for a much-needed full spa.

"Everybody dies happy here," the captain was musing to himself. But at the dice table came a shout of "No!" as one of the human-looking guests had lost his last 50 credits on an unwise bet. He was led away by an android.

Arthur and Alice watched and waited. Finally, they noticed their hope: faulty slot machines, old computers, and over-used pieces of furniture were not incinerated like paper, but thrown into a vast eject chamber and released into space. But the eject chamber was guarded by androids: no one was meant to avoid cryogenic preservation, as a strict policy, for the integrity of the empire against undesirable rebels. But the last clear-headed survivors of The Rogue were of superior intelligence, and would not be thwarted. They donned their old space-suits and approached the two android guards.

"We are androids 512 and 349," said Alice with the universal translator, "and are here to investigate the possible presence of an unknown space virus. We must enter the eject chamber."

"We were not informed," one of the androids replied.

"It's a secret, so that we don't alarm the guests," said Arthur. "Time is of the essence. We must know where the virus came from, so a full investigation must be conducted. Stand away from the door while I decontaminate. He removed from his satchel a bottle of complimentary cologne from their suite.

The two androids were hesitant, as various gel-packs vied with each other with conflicting imperatives. Then they stepped aside. Arthur sprayed the cologne imperiously as the door slid open. "This will only take several hours," he stated. Arthur and Alice entered the eject chamber, and made themselves comfortable in old stuffed chairs.

"We haven't much hope," said Alice. They tethered themselves together, and waited. In a few hours, the outer hatch slid open, and they were shot out into space with the junk. They had a limited supply of oxygen, but even death was preferable to a possibly eternal sleep. They had kept their journals. As they drifted away from The Bounty, Alice wrote:

"Before I lay me down to rest,
May the Dove of Peace enter my breast,
Lull me into a gentle sleep,
Even as I sink into the unknown deep,
And, mayhap, death, like a white scorpion,
Take my last life in dying breath.
Who doth my soul to keep?
Were life simple, not so complex,
I would stand firm, and pass the test,
And vote once for the Dove of Peace,
That death be an illusion, at the end,
And to Heaven my humble soul be sent,
Although on a one-way journey Hell-bent.
Life's illusions are yet well-meant,
And though we know not what it send,
Already I am on the mend,
And though I breath my last,
The moment shall be over fast.

Let me say, I shall not tempt the past,
Nor the future defend,
But only the moment in between,
Where I find my true best friend.
Moments pass, like a garden to tend:
May I cheat death, though verily in the Abyss,
It happened once, so I know this:
What seems like fate is Heaven's tryst."

Just when their oxygen supply was almost depleted, there came a radio transmission in their helmets: "I detected your heat signatures in the flotsam. Hot damn! You must be desperate! I'll rendezvous in just a few moments." All of a sudden, a spacecraft pulled alongside, of modest size yet made of gold. Levers reached out and grasped the stranded pair.

They were brought aboard a craft full of alien plant-life, and confronted by the larger-than-life features of a single, tall individual, wearing a green hunters costume. "'Aces' Dagon" he introduced himself cheerily. "'Luckiest man in the galaxy.' I've won at the Wheel of Fortune thirteen times, and cheated death. So it was the least I could do for you. Say, you don't look like you're from these parts...either way, you're on the lam, hoping to be rescued from space junk. You're lucky I came along..."

"Pleased to meet you," Arthur replied. "Luck had everything to do with it. We've cheated death twice, and we don't know why or how. But this seems to be a lucky quadrant of the galaxy..."

"It's that black hole, you see," said "Aces" Dagon, with some consternation. "It portends death, yet seems to create coincidence. Eventually, though, its gravity well will leave no ship untouched. That's why I got this special ship transformed by the black market for thousands of credits. I'm not waiting for fate, I'm headed to the furthest star. My gambling days have just begun..."

Alice day-dreamed of distant earth, lost now in space, but without regret. She eyed Dagon suspiciously, though, as he seemed too overt in his mannerisms. But she had a pressing question: "When will there be cryogenic defrosting? We left several friends behind."

"Cryogenic defrosting has not been perfected," came Dagon's reply, and his mood shifted to one of irony. "A single think tank is occupied with the matter, mainly composed of androids, but with a few select scientists. Freezing would be a good idea, except Cygnus is running low on time. Whoever wakes up from the deep-freeze must survive the black hole. The old 'rock and the hard place.'"

"We left the captain of our vessel," Arthur said, "back aboard The Bounty. Can he be emancipated?"

"Well, no," Dagon answered truthfully. "But I can transfer a few thousand credits into his account, make things easier for him, if he isn't unlucky."

"We also wish to emancipate two frozen colleagues," Alice said hopefully.

"A raid, eh? That hasn't happened in years. The androids far outnumber the sentients. It's a fool's errand...still, we could make a swift move of it, then jump to light speed before they're hardly aware we were there. The Bounty keeps its deep-freeze units on the starboard side. The alarms will sound, but one quick incision and we're in. We won't have time to rescue your captain, though, I'm afraid...his destiny is the black hole." He directed his golden craft verbally to head towards The Bounty. "Always gamble with life," he said as a motto.

Alice Baker wrote in her journal:

"Twice death was close, I could almost taste it,

This passing life, do not waste it!

Dare we make mention,

Of so dishonorable a detention,

That barely have we observed,

Then death is close, and has us unnerved,

And if I could give my best advice,

Cheat death not once but twice,

And down that hidden corridor,

Find everlasting life, which death opposed,

Like a door that opens, then is closed.

As sure as life hangs by a folly,

Hold life dear, be jolly, and with good cheer.

A day may last a year,

Or a year a day,

But do not let death have the final say.

Rather, live for posterity,

Which is granted as sweet charity."

The author Jeremy Steifveider longed to be free of his family. He had boarded the Orient Express bound for Istanbul. It was the cusp of the Victorian era, the beginnings of modern socialism and psychology. But Jeremy Steifveider's muse was philosophy, which his family couldn't understand. Theories of superhumanhood were just beginning. He would take a long vacation in Istanbul, he planned, and settle down to do some writing. He relaxed presently in the plush dining car with a whisky sour.

At last, Istanbul spread out before him like a Xanadu of mosques and tea-gardens. The Bosphorus River flowed past as he sat with another whisky sour in the district of the Blue Mosque. He knew his mind. He was sharp as a whip. But other people he disdained, in his native Berlin, but he was hoping all that would be different in Istanbul. At least, his Arabic was fluent. He wrote in his journal:

"At no time in history did man agree. We are by our natures contentious. What can be agreed upon are the basic instinctual drives of the human animal: the need for self-control, the desire to love, and the more primitive instincts of desiring money, food, and sexuality. Of all of the above, the instinct for self-control is primary, it dominates our conscience even when we are at rest, it shapes and molds our actions, for without it we are lost in the Dark Night of the Soul, in the primitive, in the Abyss. If man were to wake up from his dream of self-control, he would find himself an animal inchoate. Already contentious, he is bound to his fate: to overcome himself, he would lose his self-control, and be bound for the proverbial psychological guillotine. Yet paradoxically it is the only path to transcendence, and redemption for the soul, to discover the meaning of freedom. Ironically, the tendency for self-transcendence is also the tendency for self-destruction. Will man lose his soul and revert to the animal state?

"Another whisky sour," said the Baron von Steifveider. "On the rocks." He looked about him at the mingled crowd of natives and ex-patriots, a few of them in light conversation, some playing chess and backgammon. "Here I can be free," he thought to himself, "and write." He lit his pipe.

"Press that button in five seconds," "Aces" Dagon ordered Arthur. A laser made a circular incision in the starboard side of The Bounty. Cryogenic units shot into the vacuum of space.

"There! I think I see Sophia!" cried Alice, pointing.

'There's Marie!" Arthur replied excitedly. "We've found them."

"I'll haul those two in," said Dagon, "and the rest the androids can clean up. Now all we need is a civilization that can defrost the poor bastards."

"They were both dead," commented Alice hollowly.

"Nothing is as expensive as death," returned "Aces" Dagon.

"It was space sickness, so perhaps it's not too bad," Arthur said optimistically.

The two freezer units were hauled aboard by electronic arms. "The Bounty" was navigating into an offensive posture.

"Ready or not!" exclaimed Dagon, and he pressed the warp drive lever downward. "Ladies and gentlemen, the stars await!" The stars became streaks, but the gyroscopic equilibrium of "The Space Pirate" maintained. Arthur and Alice watched a counter without comprehension. They broke free of the black hole and shot towards destiny. They shot through Ursa Minor, but quarantine beacons were blinking. "Nuclear incident, probably," Dagon commented. "That's no place to be." Then, autopilot took over, sounding its signal. The three rushed to the window. Along the port side was the "U.S.S. Beagle."

"We're going home!" said Arthur, confounded. Alice and he had wished to escape earth, yet now earth, by default, by luck, by fate, would be their home again.

"Welcome to Deep Space Quadrant Ten," came the voice of the admiral of "The Beagle." "We are a peaceful people. Please identify yourselves."

"The Space Pirate," said Dagon.

"The Rogue," said Alice.

"In any event, you are welcome aboard," the admiral replied.

The Rigellian in the Star Lounge nursed his rum. His blue reptilian skin began to turn green like a chameleon. "I don't like you," he stated to "Aces" Dagon.

"That'll be three ducats," Dagon returned, putting away the cards.

The admiral joined them. "Johnson Johnson," he introduced himself, "admiral of this quadrant. We understand you have cryogenic needs. We will rendezvous with earth in two weeks at present speed. Perhaps by now they can help you."

Cryo-Organic Laboratories Director Marsha Clarke looked up with interest. "How did they die?"

"Without wounds," said Alice, "or disease, just space sickness. They were completely innocent until the end," she added.

"They may not feel the same when they wake up," said Miss Clarke. "They must be thawed from the inside out." She gestured to several proton microwave units.

"Neurotransmitters, neurochemistry, brain waves, metabolism, all may be altered...especially brain waves."

"I know Sophia," Alice interjected, "she'll make it through. But Marie, she was more delicate..."

"It may be reversed. After freezing is anybody's guess," Director Marsha Clarke replied. "Is there anything else you'd like defrosted?"

"You've melted my heart," said "Aces" Dagon.

"No dates," returned Marsha. "Just like the de-freezing process." She replaced her spectacles on her nose, adjusted her white smock, and proceeded to type.

"We can wait," said Alice. But already she was yearning to leave earth back to the stars. Soon, though, she and Arthur would have to report to NASA Mission Control.

"So you're the survivors of The Rogue," Chief Psychiatrist Lawrence Felding said with unfeigned interest. "Tell me, how do you feel?"

"A little thin," Alice replied. "It must be something I didn't eat."

The Chief Psychiatrist chuckled nervously. "And you?" he directed his question to Arthur.

"The center of the galaxy is no place to be, and Captain Patel has been lost. Still, what is one civilizations loss might be another's gain..."

"We may hope," the psychiatrist said. "Have you been experiencing any dizziness, fatigue, depression, or sleeplessness in any way?"

"Fit as a fiddle," Arthur lied. Being back on earth had given him a case of insomnia. But he wished to keep his formal standing with NASA.

"I see," said the psychiatrist. "Now we shall proceed to the spinal tap..."

The Baron Jeremiah von Steifveider sat contentedly in an Istanbul cafe, dimly lit and full of smoke. "There is no ultimate morality," he wrote, "except in action, by doing good deeds. Everything in the abstract is purely relative, and unquantified. Those who do good deeds are elevated," he continued, not knowing that he was being prescient, "into a class of extraordinary beinghood, which puts them in harmony with the universal will-to-good. This is the primary, singular fact which separates good men from great men."

The Rigellian met "Aces" Dagon in a darkened alleyway. "For your ship made of gold, I will trade you a teleportation device..." he said suggestively, his reptilian skin changing from blue to green to red. It was all the same to him, he had three more.

"A teleportation device..." Dagon mused. "It's a deal," he concluded finally.

Marie Foster awakened in a hospital bed in her hospital gown. Sophia Price was in the next bed, busily consuming some lasagna.

"Where are we?" asked Marie.

"Don't care," said Sophia. "We're back on earth."

"I don't feel so well," said Marie.

"Have some lasagna," Sophia replied.

In walked Arthur and Alice, with Dagon accompanying them. "You're both looking well," Arthur lied. They were both as pale as sheets.

"For someone who died," Sophia enjoined.

"That's why I don't feel well," Marie said. She still had space sickness.

"Try the chicken salad," Sophia suggested.

"What was it like?" asked Alice. "We came close to death ourselves."

"I was completely unconscious," said Sophia Price.

"I saw lights," Marie Foster replied. "They were beautiful."

"It's all in your head," said Sophia.

"Everything is," commented Dagon.

Alice took some time away to write:

"When the young bird she first awoke,

And like Heaven, like springtime, first she spoke,

She sang of life, not of the past,

But a springtime that would always last.

And I asked the bird, 'what immortal melody,

Doth thou now relate to me?'

And she said, 'the song is of the First Light,

Which ever fades into the night,

But promises springtime, and the warm robins breast,

Which beats with a heart ever-blessed.

When one bird dies, alone, without a cry,

You can hear Heaven itself moan and sigh,

And it is possessed, again, by a little birds loveliness,

Even as the image of the Most High,

Which comes in springtime, natures guest.'

And the little bird confessed,

In the sweet by-and-by,

'I sing because I know I will fly.'"

"When do we go back to space?" asked Sophia Price of Alice Baker.

"I don't feel so well," moaned Marie Foster. "I think I'll just lie in bed."

"The Beagle debarks again in two weeks," said Alice. "We'll all go."

"I just want to grow daisies," said Marie Foster.

The Beagle lifted off from the Presidio in San Francisco. Soon Earth lay below, with metropolis's glowing like constellations. The Star Lounge was packed with sight-seers, who were onboard to see Jupiter up close. After cruising mildly for half an hour, The Beagle stood before the gas giant, which filled the window of the lounge.

"I've got to go," explained "Aces" Dagon to the others. "I've had some more good luck, and got my hands on a teleportation device. All I need to do is press several buttons, and the galaxy will lie at my feet."

Alice decided to compose an ode:
"When out of the forest, at night,
The mockingbird takes its flight,
Though wings be heavy, the song is light.
Whenever I look up to the sky,
I question God and ask him, 'Why?'
In all the immensity of the tremendous Throne,
Are little men still left alone?
And if just one man dares take flight,
Like the mockingbird, when does the song
Cease to be heard?
Which star is his that shown?
Ever since Orville and Wilbur Wright,
We take to the sky, reach the vast unknown,
Before we're even ready grown.
And the astronomers they say, 'Beware!'

Do not approach too quickly,
Heaven's bending, winding stair,
As you glide through nebulas, shining, fair.
You will find yourself with the Lion, the Bear,
Who come out from their hidden lair,
And challenge any dare with dare.
Do not go too quick, too slow,
For what is waiting there?
A circus of a starry, gleaming show,
But the stars they do not care,
And one life may a great world make,
It is only for man to know,
And his destiny awaits to slake,
Beyond the stars that glow."

"Aces" Dagon went back to his quarters aboard The Beagle and unearthed the teleportation device from his luggage. "This side up," it read in Rigellian. His co-conspirator had shown him how to press different series of buttons to arrive in different quadrants of the galaxy. The device contained more than 500 M-class planets. He pointed the beaming end towards himself and clicked. But the Rigellian had sold him damaged goods. A malfunction occurred, and "Aces" Dagon disappeared into the past, and was replaced aboard The Beagle by one Jeremy Steifveider, who, sitting calmly in a tea-garden in Istanbul, had been beamed up by Dagon. Below The Beagle on planet earth, World War III had broken out, and all sides had lost. Earth was in ruins. The space-fleet was all that was left of humanity. "Aces" Dagon, "the luckiest man in the galaxy," sat in Istanbul at the turn of the 20th century, with a whisky sour poised in front of him. The descendants of the superhuman would upset the balance of the race, even as earth would miss the Baron Jeremiah von Steifveider, sharp as a whip, and his critical role in Earths destiny. With this replacement, Earth realized a shattering paradox.

"There's something drastically wrong," the first mate reported to Admiral Johnson Johnson. "We get no response from NASA."

"Code grey," the admiral responded immediately.

CygnusX1 was crushed into the black hole with a terrific supernovae. Androids went scrambling, as one by one, their ships were drawn into the gravity well. Alexandro Patel had survived, luckily, for many a year, playing baccarat. Now, there was mutiny on "The Bounty." Sentients grappled with androids in a futile attempt to board another craft. Captain Alexandro Patel merely sat and nursed his blue raspberry margarita. "Tell me truly, have I gone mad?" he asked to no-one in particular. The Bounty was crushed like paper by the black hole. The center of the galaxy was devoured by an infinite appetite.

"Aces" Dagon knew something was wrong. All the spacecraft were missing. "I must be in the past," he mused with irony. And he did not speak Arabic. "I must take a wife, finally," he concluded as his only course of action.

Jeremy Steifveider gazed in awe at Jupiter filling his window. "This is not supposed to be," he thought with nervous dread. He lit his pipe and tried to settle down reflectively. He wrote in his journal: "If man knew his future, he would always regret his past. For every action there is a reaction, and only a magic mirror can see all ends. Man should fight and tear and claw his way through life, and not be a sedentary shrew. Our destiny is in the stars, yet who would know to take life by the horns, and forge a future, in this pain-wracked universe. Little do we suspect, as we lead our simple lives, the complexity we are shielded from." His tobacco smoke filled the room, and fans initiated themselves automatically. "But to become a part of this complexity is what is most desirable, though we rarely see the means for the end, we only guess, and then try to play right. Every man is bound to regrettable decisions. For myself, I have been drawn into the New Life, unexpectedly."

"The Challenger" made docking procedures with The Beagle. "Earth is destroyed," the captain reported to Admiral Johnson Johnson. "Only the lunar colony now survives. We must consider every action, and abrogate fate."

"We are caught in a temporal paradox," the admiral concluded, "but if it happened once it can happen again. We must find the Chosen."

Jeremy Steifveider finally crept from his quarters to the Star Lounge. "A whisky sour," he intoned to the bartender.

Sophia Price looked at him boldly from the next barstool. Marie Foster joined them and ordered a tonic. Her space sickness was at last wearing off. An announcement came across the intercom from the admiral. "We have crossed through a rift in time. Earth lies in our past, destroyed. But let me assure all you welcome guests, that we have not been abandoned by fate. All who wish to debark on the moon are free to do so. For those wishing to return to earth, my deepest sympathy." The admiral ordered quarantine beacons to be released.

Alice Baker joined them at the bar, with Arthur Wright in tow. Jeremy von Steifveider looked utterly refined in his period costume and broad-rimmed hat. He stroked his goatee in wonderment.

"And what is your name?" Alice asked. Jeremy admired her thin beauty.

"I used to be called Jeremy by my parents. Now you may call me what you like. As long as it isn't an insult."

"Jeremy is nice," said Alice mildly.

"I saw him first," said Sophia, growing cross.

The Rigellian approached for his rum. His skin turned from blue to orange. Jeremy Steifveider looked on in horror, terrified, mortified.

"You destroyed earth," he observed acutely.

"A deceptively simple thing to do," the Rigellian replied. "One rum, straight," he added.

"We must report you to the admiral," returned Jeremy.

"There's nothing to say," the Rigellian stated flatly. "What's done is done, and I cannot be held accountable. You have mere words."

"Every word is important," Jeremy Steifveider countered.

Admiral Johnson Johnson heard the case. "According to NASA imperatives, the only method to undo a paradox is to replace what originally went wrong with what should have been." He looked at Jeremy with great interest. "I have never met anybody from the past, but if what you say is true, we must seal the Rigellian's quarters and investigate. Hope here is a slender thread."

"It was 'Aces' Dagon," Alice remarked. "He said he had a teleportation device, and this is when Jeremy appeared. They may have replaced each other. In theory, Dagon creates World War III and Jeremy prevents it. Our mission, or at least those who decide to take it, must be to murder Dagon and replace him with Jeremy..."

"We must prevent this Dagon from having offspring..." concluded the admiral.

"In the Rigellian's quarters was discovered his three extra teleportation devices. Expert technological analysts were drawn from the crew, including Alice Baker. At first, the machines looked merely like touch-pad computers. But their suspicions were alerted when one of the objects disappeared into thin air, leaving only two mysterious cryptograms.

On earth, Dagon still had his remote device, but was busy earning money at backgammon. He could not resist a good game of dice. And he still thought it was a good place to get married, as good a place as any. He was tall and rugged, and looked European. Surely, he thought, an ex-patriate of some sort could be lured to him. What he didn't know was that time was subject to humans, rather than humans subject to time.

After months of analysis, Alice declared, "It's these three buttons, and we must hurry." The admiral, Alice, Arthur, Sophia, Marie, and Jeremy von Steifveider were all gathered together to decide a momentous fate: who would accompany Jeremy back in time, risking the consequences. Alice was deemed the most fit by consensus.

"You must wear period costume, and take only money and the time machines, one each, with you," said Admiral Johnson Johnson. "What happens to your future earth will depend on you. Find Dagon, but be careful, very careful, of what you do. He is in Istanbul, as we theorize. God-speed, and may earth receive mercy."

"We'll miss you," Arthur said. "Cheat death again, for our sakes and yours. And never look back."

With just the touch of a few buttons Baron Jeremiah von Steifveider and Alice Baker were sitting in a tea-garden by the Bosphorus River. But Dagon was nowhere to be seen. He had finished playing backgammon and had gone to a local tavern with his winnings.

"Time is of the essence. What do we do now?" Alice asked.

"Time may be on our side," replied Jeremy. "We may have years to find this Dagon fellow. You say he stands out in a crowd."

"We must be more forensic than that. Ask the waiter if they've seen him."

"He walked in that direction, after winning at backgammon," the waiter replied to Jeremy in Arabic." It was the direction of the train station.

"C'mon," said Alice, shivering. "His trail is already growing cold."

"First I must purchase a pistol," Jeremy responded, "and if he's the man I think he is, he has stopped for a drink somewhere."

"You must be mad!" Captain Alexandro Patel almost shouted at First Mate Alice Baker. The rest of the crew peered at the argument with blank, cryogenic stares from their refrigerator units. The distant stars looked on upon their tiny vessel. They had gone beyond sixteen billion years from the center of the universe. They were beyond the oldest galaxy and only one last star cluster remained confronting them.

"It cannot be debated," returned Alice Baker. "Your Magnetic Resonance Imaging scan reveals too much bone loss." In addition, the captain of "The Unicorn" was experiencing extreme space sickness, and was rapidly decompensating psychologically. He looked around him for a weapon, and saw a laser.

"Don't move!" he declared. "I swear I'll use it!"

"Captain, be reasonable," Alice tried as a last resort. But the captain was stubborn to the last. He aimed the laser at her head. Alice could barely think on her feet quick enough, and reached out desperately and grabbed a mirror. The ruby laser ricocheted back into the captains left eye, sending piercing neuro-retinal feedback deep into his brain, into his hippocampus. Alice pushed him backwards into one of the five cryogenic freezing units and locked the capsule. At long last, she was alone. She managed to relax, and smile with self-satisfaction. Her bone density was normal. Her only obstacle would be to make it back to earth, to earths far-flung future. So far, the ships operational procedures seemed normal. Infrared telescopes continued to take movies, some of which she watched on the view-scope. Below her, the oldest galaxy in the universe glared darkly. She turned to writing in her journal, her quixotic poetry:

"The jester was a fool, they say,
But in his wisdom had his say,
And the stars were his clear, abundant token,
Far above the silver Milky Way,

With a destiny awoken,
To change the dark night to payne's grey.
For the jester he had spoken,
'Riddle me this, riddle me that,
Of Fomalhaut obscured by bats,
Of Polaris, perhaps still standing there unshaken,
As the Great Bear and Little Bear sat,
With the Dog Star now turned into a black cat,
Which confounded the wise men from afar,
As they followed, wandering, each wandering star,
With Scorpius, still a hideous sting,
Riddle me of the inconstant things,
Where only devils tread,
A ball of yarn unravelling,
Until, at long last, we are dead.'
The jester knew of what tomorrow brings,
And so he plucks at his lute, and ever so quietly
sings,

For what is wisdom, with such inconstant kings?
The stars yet shine, throughout the day,
Their light hidden by the sun,
As though Sol plays, but is bidden,
To blot out life from the sky, like a chariot ridden,
And a wise man might question, "Why?"
The stars are yet awake, some treason,
And good stars die, without a reason,
As fragile as galaxies, colliding in their season,
While earth looks on, seemingly abiding,
But spins and wobbles in its attempt at hiding,
Hiding from the question, 'Why?'
Which lets stars live, but God to die."

Alice Baker had joined "The Unicorn" on their quest for the beginnings of the universe, of "Why?" "How long should I remain her?" she pondered to herself. No one at NASA had known whether or not other rockets would appear beyond the oldest galaxy. It was a risk she would endure for only so long before folding space again and returning to earth's future. Already she had been away millennia.

She turned her attention to the frozen crew. Marie Foster's eyes were the brightest, but Alice knew she was delicate, and the results of defrosting were always uncertain. Sophia Price's dark eyes appeared hostile and unrelenting. Arthur Wright looked entirely innocent, as usual.

She had to make a command decision. She turned off the life support for Captain Alexandro Patel and for Sophia Price. The other two, Marie and Arthur, she would let live. As Chief Psychiatrist and character analyst for the mission, it was her best decision, as otherwise every one of the five-member crew would have to be defrosted before earth-time, and there were too many risks and uncertainties. She would take only so many risks, even if it meant playing the Angel of Death itself, Abaddon.

The Baron Jeremiah von Steifveider had purchased Europe from the Ukraine to the Rock of Gibraltar. He was the dominant cause of world peace and economic stability. His primary industries were gardening and robots. He sat in a quiet drawing-room in his castle in Liechtenstein, with fresh air pouring in with the morning sunlight, deeply engrossed in a chess game with Sophia Price the 10th, a dark beauty with gleaming black eyes whom he was considering proposing to. The chief chef arrived to take their orders. No intercoms were used in the castle.

"I'll have breakfast number one hundred eleven," said Jeremy. "What will you be having, Sophia, my dear?"

"Give me Spain," she replied, only half-joking. "Check-mate in five," she added.

Neither Marie Foster nor Arthur Wright had sufficient bone density for their safety until The Unicorn once again reached the Sol Quadrant. Alice would awaken them then. She had decided, in her prudence, not to remain in her present vector much longer. Then, as rapidly as a bullet, a sleek dark craft like a submarine appeared besides The Unicorn. Alice pulled the lever for sub-space folding and didn't look back, lest she be turned into a pillar of salt. But she had doubts this curse could be avoided. She had gone too far, she mused.

"Aces" Dagon was so drunk on Russian vodka he could barely walk straight. He took his remaining backgammon winnings and headed for The Blue House Hotel for an inexpensive room. Dusk was falling rapidly, and Venus was shining in the last glow of the sunset. "Tomorrow I'll find a bride," he thought tipsily.

Alice and Jeremy were following him up the street. Jeremy had his pistol in his pocket. "Remember what the admiral said, we must be careful, very careful. Let's first see where he goes." They followed at a discreet distance, and reached The Blue House Hotel.

Dagon first ordered another drink at the bar. Alice and Jeremy sat behind newspapers in the lobby. "Aces"

Dagon then proceeded to the lobby counter for a room. Alice and Jeremy listened intently.

"Here's room 418. Up the stairs and to your left." Dagon exited the lobby, swerving slightly. Alice and Jeremy waited. A bell rang. "Room service ordered for room 418," a bell-hop was told.

Alice knocked. "Room service," she said. The door opened, and Jeremy shot Dagon in the head. His body remained standing for an instant with an uncomprehending stare. His luck had run out. Jeremy pushed him over and closed the door behind them. They would await room service.

The U.S.S Beagle floated high above a peaceful earth. "Ladies and gentlemen," Admiral Johnson Johnson declared, "we may now go home again!"

Alice Baker watched the universes oldest galaxy pass by on her telemetry monitor. Her old sense of deja vu was acting up. The rest of the crew was cryogenically preserved. She decided, in the uncertainty of her recurrent deja vu, to wake up Arthur.

He blinked blearily and rubbed his eyes. "Where are we? What time is it?" he queried Alice.

"We've reached destination," replied Alice, "but I'm having disturbing doubts about the time."

"Space is so bent with gravity, it probably doesn't matter," he joked with a double-entendre. She cheered up.

"Arthur, it's good to see you..."

"It's good to see you, Alice." She was looking somewhat thin, but still very beautiful.

The last stars faded behind them, and they entered the void of Deep Space aboard "The Argonaut." A few last solitary asteroids passed by in an instant. They were entirely alone, or so they thought.

Sophia Price the 10th looked at Jeremy closely, fearing she had said too much. Jeremy guarded his immortality.

"Room service!" came a female's voice outside room 418.

"I'll get it," Alice said. She and Jeremy greedily consumed a Lebanese buffet. "Should we go or should we stay?" she asked Jeremy with her mouth full.

"This is my era, my home. Perhaps you should use your device before it dematerializes." Alice Baker wanted to stay with Jeremy, but the ramifications of being out of time were too great. They had been sent as a pair only as a fail-safe clause, that if one should fail the other might succeed. They had met with success quickly, be it meaningful coincidence or sheer good fortune. "Never tempt fate." Jeremy looked out the window at Algol, al-Ghul. "The universe is haunted," he concluded acutely. "We must be going. He desperately wanted Alice to stay, but was willing to lose love. The pair left The Blue House Hotel and wandered down to the docks of the Bosphorus River. They found an open tea-garden. "A whisky sour, on the rocks," Jeremy said.

"Tea, please," said Alice. It was nearly midnight. Istanbul sparkled with lamp-light. They fell silent, and wrote in their respective journals. Jeremy wrote, as usual, about philosophy, and Alice poetry:

"If all our sins could be repaid,
We would not once have tarried, never strayed,
By that great river, under the Milky Way,
For time is short, unless you make a trade,

With myriad stars, where destiny doth lay.

Come tomorrow, come what may,

Thou shalt meet thy sorrow, after many a fine day,

As Algol, in the night, doth prey

Upon sweet lovers, whose love turns grey,

As your distant star has the final say.

Beware! For certain stars became fey

Long before the earth turned and held its sway."

"Let's awake the others now," Arthur suggested. "If they need to be put to sleep again, it probably can be risked..." Deep Space expanded before The Argonaut, but in their slip-stream they were catching up with the boundaries of the known universe.

"Okay," said Alice, "but remember they may be delicate. We can risk it, though," she decided. But every decision might have unknown echoes. Marie Foster was too delicate, and died in the defrosting procedure. However, Captain Alexandro Patel and Sophia Price survived.

"Where are we?" the captain immediately inquired.

"In the great north-west," Alice replied. "Captain, Marie didn't make it."

"We must carry on, and not look back," the captain said curtly, stubbornly. "Not until we know what lies beyond space..."

"Perhaps it is another space," put in Arthur. "Or a place where our imagination would fail us." The Argonaut was rapidly losing telemetry.

"We might lose ourselves in the night," said Alice. "We're losing stars to guide us by."

"Man is greater than the stars," replied the captain with a certain hubris. "The Holy Grail of astronomy and human endeavor lies before us..."

"I really feel rather small," said Arthur.

"Perhaps you should be put to sleep," said the captain unexpectedly.

The Argonaut ceased detecting the universal background radiation, yet they were still in space.

The Baron Jeremiah von Steifveider decided not to marry Sophia Price the 10th. He had discovered she knew a Rigellian. But beyond that, he was sensing, acutely, significant alterations in her behavior, as though her patience with something was growing thin. He sensed that that something was him.

"Well," she asked him one day, "when will you marry me?"

"I've decided I'm not the marrying type," he lied. He sensed something was desperately wrong. He decided it was best to produce his old Istanbul pistol. Time-travel had made him immortal, but that could be abrogated by any physical means. He sensed she was carrying a weapon of her own, by a nervousness she attempted vainly to conceal. "My decision is final. My decision is life." He fired one silver bullet through her heart. He looked down in sympathy at her corpse. "From earth ye came. Earth will receive you back." He felt like hell.

Jeremy sat with Alice in the streaming morning sun by the Bosphorus River. "I think I must be going," she said finally.

"I think so, too," he replied with regret. "Anomalies must be avoided at all cost, if possible. Fair thee well, wherever, and whenever, you may be. If ever it be so, that on another sunny day, we meet, I shall consider myself blessed."

"May you always know happiness," she warmly replied.

"Arthur was down on one knee. "Will you marry me, Alice?" he asked plaintively, producing a ring he had saved all this time.

"Arthur," Alice said, "don't you think we should give it more time?"

Captain Alexandro Patel had overheard. "Don't be a fool, Arthur," he said boisterously, although he, himself, secretly intended to marry Sophia Price.

"I wish things could be different..." Arthur commented sadly.

Just then, the alarm sounded. The telescopes had detected a distant light in the Abyss. "We're home, at last," the captain declared mistakenly. "Novus Ordo Seclorum!"

"We have found the Grail," Sophia repeated.

"We go slow," said First Mate Alice Baker. Swiftly, the Chief Psychiatrist inoculated the captain with a knock-out dosage of morphine. "He goes back in the freezer," she attempted to explain to the other two.

"Traitor!" screamed Sophia. "Give me that needle!"

"You have space sickness," replied Alice mildly, "and so did he."

Sophia reached out for Alice's throat, but fortunately Arthur found a blunt object, the ships only paperweight, and decided the matter with a quick stroke to the back of Sophia Price's skull. Alice and Arthur put the captain and Sophia back into their cryogenic freezer units.

"We stop here and wait," Alice pronounced, "or tempt fate."

"Or fate is already tempted," Arthur responded with fright.

A sleek black craft like a submarine pulled alongside The Argonaut.

"Prepare to be boarded," rasped the universal translator.

"Backwards!" cried Alice. But it was too late: The Argonaut was in the unyielding grip of a magnetic tractor ray. "Self-destruct!" she yelled once more, and pulled the correct lever. The Argonaut flared briefly in space with nuclear fission. The other craft was obliterated into a million black pieces, which drifted noiselessly into the void.

The Red Flag of war had been raised.

Alice Baker woke up in the medical bay on board the U.S.S Beagle, with Admiral Johnson Johnson and Marie Foster by her side. Sophia Price was noticeably absent.

"How was Istanbul?" Admiral Johnson Johnson queried. "By the way, you have a clean bill of health, and are now a renowned hero."

"I left Jeremy," was all she would say. She ate a full meal, hungrily. Then she dressed from hospital gown into her formal NASA uniform, and went to her quarters. There, she wrote a note to Marie Foster: "Dearest Marie: be happy wherever you go. I now know where I must go. Perhaps, one day, we will meet again. Love, Alice." The teleportation device was still lying on her desk. She studied it intently, pressed several buttons, and prayed.

Jeremy von Steifveider decided to leave his castle in Liechtenstein and return to his beloved Istanbul, even though he didn't own it. He felt he needed rest and relaxation, and to write more again. He took a suite aboard the Orient Express, and took out his journal:

"Life's little plagues are that we are not mindful. Life should be a food chewed slowly, like cud. Then we should write. Every man and woman is a book. Every word should be golden."

The Bosphorus gleamed under a hot sun. It was many millennia since he had enjoyed Istanbul, where his heart was broken, but this time he was mysteriously drawn there. But he worried about the past as much as the future. Would there be another paradigm shift? He still kept his teleportation device, but dared not use it.

Just as the ebony submarine craft had been obliterated beyond Deep Space, the known universe was obliterated from all sides in retaliation. The immense might of the black holes exerted themselves into crushing the stars, one by one, into supernovae. But that was in Jeremy's distant past. Earth still floated below its sun, magically, a crystal ball teeming with life.

Jeremy sat down in his old favorite tea-garden in the Blue Mosque district.

"A whisky sour, please, on the rocks," he said in fluent Arabic.

"Jeremy! My love!" cried Alice. "I've found you!" It was only several hours since they had parted.

"My Alice! I've never forgotten you!" They hugged each other warmly. "How ironic! How playful! How wonderful is life!" he proclaimed.

But the deepest irony was that The Argonaut had not yet set sail.

Alice had to sit down and write:

"Two things doth this story tell:

Man is made of Heaven, and Man is made of Hell.

The days are sunny,

While around the world tolls midnights bell.

Reason once, then reason again,

As on this little ball you spin,

And second-guess your actions, then.

Do not fall prey to mere fabrications.

Abandon strife! Find elations,

For as long as last the constellations

In your eye: but beware of the old question, 'Why?'

For two things made of art thou and I."

CHAPTER EIGHTEEN:
The Big Crunch

Far, far away in time and space, further than we can imagine, lay, starless, the Outer Satellites. Slowly they had become populated, as a migration from the super-heated menace of the stars had begun. People from many races coexisted peacefully in the dark of night, their holograms providing them with enough for everybody. But eventually there was overcrowding, and the Outer Satellites shut their doors to new-comers.

All was quiet. Yet over time, their children would grow up bigger than they.

"This is my place in line," Delta 5 said to Amrita.

"I was here first," she complained. The food service replicator line was crowded that hour.

"You don't belong here," Delta 5 rejected.

"I'll report this to the superintendent!" Amrita replied defiantly. "This is no place for bullies!"

"You can say what you want. Anarchy is a growing movement, day by day more are learning about freedom."

"We already have freedom," she returned. "I do nothing all day but paint."

"That is not real freedom. Ours is not an ethic, but a code." He did not give up his place in the line. "For the greater good a real government should be set in place."

"I'm leaving," Amrita stated flatly.

But Delta 5 had other plans. He produced a large space rock, and struck Amrita squarely and strongly on the back of her head. Murder had come to paradise.

The crowd in line stood stunned, except those in the know. A few people jumped on Delta 5, but with his superior strength he shrugged them off. "I'll be in my quarters," he proclaimed to the throng. "After I get my food." there were brief quotes of rebellion, dismay, and disbelief, but no further challengers. Death had not afflicted the Outer Satellites for generations. The assembled people could barely recognize it. Some children, however, had grown bigger than their creators.

"The people said you did this," Superintendent Abodé claimed.

"I do not know who did it,' Delta 5 denied.

"There were many eye-witnesses. Do you not fear the Nameless One?" said the superintendent of God.

"Moralizing and philosophizing are the devices of the deluded," Delta 5 said plainly.

"We don't know what to do with you," the superintendent advised. "We can't let you stay, and we can't exactly let you leave, either. As all the Satellites are full, we will give you your own isolation dome on one of our surfaces. You will live there unbothered for the rest of your life. You will have your own replicator."

Delta 5 became a mythological hero to some, who had hardened their hearts against the captivity they had been born into. He replicated in his dome paper and pen, and would write his code for whomever might find it or release him. Dissent began to foment. Leisure bred contempt, and contempt bred strife, and eventually strife bred anarchy. Following their imprisoned hero, twenty candidates for similar immortality founded a scheme of vengeance.

During dinner seating one evening, forks and knives were used as weapons. Before the riot could be quelled, over fifty were dead in the mayhem. Four of the perpitrators disappeared during the melee. The rest ended up in their own isolation domes, peering at the vague lights of distant galaxies. They, too, would write for posterity.

"I would like to request our profiles be revised," the superintendent said to his only secretary. "Additionally, we shall make more replicators, one for every room, and when we have we shall enforce a bed alert."

"How do we do that?" queried the secretary, adjusting her skirt uncomfortably.

"By concensus, I believe," replied the super.

The glass of Shanghai shown brilliantly as massive towers and pyramids. But down one small lane was a little old brick building, an Episcopalian church. Two missionaries stood humbly by the pool of water. Their infant was dipped by the reverend. "And what shall she be called?" he asked them.

The female missionary spoke. "She shall be called Lisbeth. Lisbeth Elkhorn."

"So be it."

Tremendous solar flares lit the sky with extra heat. The sun was dying, and after wars, plagues, famines, and exiles the human race was finally prepared for space migration. Lisbeth Elkhorn's parents would be missionaries. The rest of the crew of that ship was reserved for scientists with physical prowess. Lisbeth would be the only baby, and the last to survive.

They were to head away from their home galaxy, which burned furiously with spectacular novaes. They would reach for the void, and whatever mysteries it might contain.

Robert Elkhorn cooked dinner, while Lisbeth was bottle-fed a special solution by Diana. Lisbeth's birth-weight had been low.

Sol faded as a distant gleam. The respective scientists, all four thousand plus, labored away, deep in their calculations. The ship was rapidly gaining speed, with its anti-matter propulsion.

Lisbeth started to cry. She remembered back to the birth canal, but was still caught in the dream of infancy, the "preconscious" for most people. Their ship was one of many which were all sent in different directions with different crew components. Lisbeth's ship, "The Artful Dodger," would eventually have an elderly crew. But it had the finest scientists of the day working on their calculations. Their hopes were pinned on Lisbeth. She would be the sole survivor eventually, after they reached a stable star system that still had an M-class planet, many years away. The galaxies were being sucked, inevitably, into their black holes.

But Lisbeth's eyes glowed green, like the green hills of Earth. She was surrounded by many books. And the food was excellent. She always felt hungry, for more books as well as more food. But there were no other children to play with. She roamed the corridors under neon lights. The rest of the crew always said "hello," but then ignored her. But she had adoring parents. They were always doting upon her, reading her to sleep (with the lights on, because her eyes flashed with light when she was in darkness), and playing her favorite card games, and other games of chance.

Little could anyone suspect that the Outer Saellites were being pulled themselves towards "the Big Crunch." There were only slim hopes versus absolute chaos.

The intercom aboard the Artful Dodger blared one day: "Our Milky Way has collided with Andromeda. To all sentience, our prayers."

"May peace be with them," Diana Elkhorn prayed. Robert was replicating Lisbeth new clothes. The Rapture had never occured, and he was becoming increasingly agnostic for a missionary.

"Daddy," Lisbeth inquired, "why aren't there other children?" Other children she had only seen photos of.

"Every ship had to be different," explained her father. "We were lucky to get onboard at all. Always remember your good fortune." But he regreted terribly that there were no other children for her, that Mission Control had decided to make an experiment of her in this way. But it was the only way for them to get onboard and remain alive. "Your better days are ahead," he told his young daughter. Already she was smarter than the rest of the crew. She took down the crucifix from the wall.

"Do not worship graven images," she told her mother. Her mother put the crucifix in a drawer.

"Whatever you say, Lisbeth," she replied mildly. "But remember, Christ died for your sins."

"I'm only four, mama," said Lisbeth.

Robert brought her a lovely white lace dress . "It's the best the replicator has to offer." He also had downloaded black patent shoes. "You'll look the sight!"

Delta 5 was busy writing his memoir, even as the Outer Satellites were slowly being drawn towards the emassing singularity billions of light years away, the Big Crunch.

"We are not drunk on the wine of the philosophers. We do not wish to place the weak in an untenable situation, only show them the error of their ways, and offer real redemption for the mind. The mind that is pure admits its bondage, and then knows freedom. For the free, it is better to know bondage. Seek bondage and be pure. Fight, and know peace. This has already been the Way. If there is a future, it shall be shown to the way again.

"Our code does not admit error, as all error must be eradicated. The concept of free will is one of the greatest errors of all. We are all of us conditioned, yea, preconditioned, by environment and information. We live among the circumscribed boundaries of what we consider 'knowledge' and 'self-knowledge,' but cannot forever remain secure, as our self-image is derivitive of our experience. Do not forsake free will to become an automaton, do it because there is no free will. Conform only to code, not to ethic."

Satellite XK was experiencing a major breakdown in communication. For safety, the residents had to be cloistered, but the intercom was replete with conflicting sentiment. Many wished to contact another satellite. But the Superintendent Abodé deemed this might lead to further revolution by admixture. Yet, he thought, already their former lives had been circumscribed out of existence. He had originally been appointed mainly to oversee minor positive adjustments. Now the innocent denizens of his asteroid were barely living better than those in incarceration, and he was left to make the difficult decision of integration with another satellite.

"Who would want us?" he theorized.

Delta 5 peered out of his isolation dome at the distant collision of galaxies, barely a blur. "I must join another colony," he thought.

"That's it!" cried a surveillance technician, looking up from his infra-red telescope. The Artful Dodger had discovered a remote planetoid surrounded by three distant red dwarfs, stars that had already novaed. The planetoid barely had light, but it had greenery.

Captain Johnson Johnson began making preparations to reverse the anti-matter propulsion units, when suddenly two very different crafts raced by the windows of the Artful Dodger in a brief instant. One was clearly chasing the other, and their relative speed was terrific. "They'll make it," he supposed.

Superintendent Abodé watched as his satellite was drawn towards the Big Crunch. "I see something now," he reported to his secretary. "An M-class planetoid with three red dwarfs. We'll let the mercenaries off there. Perhaps it is unfair, as the spirit of anarchy might drive them to ruin. But at least we will return to a peaceful civilization for the duration." Which would not be very long. Black holes were colliding with one another, forming super-holes. Light itself could not escape, nor even the faster-than-light. Except for a very few.

The two unknown spacecraft sped past the Outer Satellites at terrific velocities, the one pursuing the other.

Lisbeth Elkhorn wandered in a dim wood of moss and mistletoe. Her parents had unfolded her own geodesic dome for her, but she was more content to wander alone. The anarchists had rebelled against each other until only Delta 5 remained alive. He wandered the same forest, hunting. He came across Lisbeth Elkhorn.

"You are of the chosen," he stated immediately.

Lisbeth Elkhorn had never met a pathology before. But at thirteen she was well-educated.

"You must be assimilated into the code," Delta 5 explained hopefully, prematurely.

Lisbeth removed a laser from her satchel and cut Delta 5 in half length-wise.

The two foreign ships sped into the night, the one hotly pursuing the other.

The rest of the universe had been sucked, inevitably, into a series of black holes, which collided and merged with ultra-powerful explosions. Finally, one tremendous gravity well reduced everything to a point. Space itself was being sucked in now, and the point hung quavering with its ineffable mass until it could not endure: it exploded with all the power of a compacted universe, hurling out matter in all directions. A breath was on the waters again.

The two ships hung, the one directly behind the other, for a few brief moments, and then disappeared.

Time began to return. But the two ships would not return for a billion years.

"Where am I?" Lisbeth complained.

Jude Underwood and Annabel Scrivenor searched her face sympathetically. "We only had supplies for one more," said Annabel. "We are now far in the future. The universe is spreading out below us. Soon, there will be an identifiable civization."

"My parents are dead!" the thirteen year old Lisbeth wailed.

"We're here to look after you," Annabel Scrivenor consoled. Deep below shone the blur of the galaxies, still new-forming.

"Annabel," Jude interrupted, "down and to the right. They're right behind us still."

Wolfgang and Claudia Mueller sat in their opulence. "They won't get away!" Wolfgang swore.

"They shall pay for their crimes!" Cauldia responded vehemently.

Sebastian and Stefan Mueller had been Co-Directors of National Intelligence. Power corrupts, but this time it did not have to. Their hearts were hardened, even as the universe was preparing for the Big Crunch. But conspiracy breeds conspiracy, and the dire race for space had been about to begin. One thing stood in its way: the brothers.

They were concealed well behind a security labyrinth dotted at various points by Earths finest commandos. But this was nothing to Jude Underwood. He used the deepest parts of his brain and simply appeared in the brothers office, sitting calmly in one of their stuffed chairs, smoking a pipe.

"You realize," he had said to Stefan, "Sebastian cannot be trusted." Stefan had long suspected his brother secretly hated him. "Neither of you shall make it onboard," Jude added. "He hates you."

"He lies!" Stefan had blurted unconvincingly.

"You lie!" came the bitter response from Sebastian. Sebastian hated Stefan and Stefan hated Sebastian, even though they were twins.

Furious, accusing stares were returned like swords between the brothers. They mutually, almost as though imitating each other, began to twitch for their lasers. They noticed the other doing so, and the matter was sealed. But the timing was to neithers advantage. Sebastian was cut through the lungs, and Stefan beheaded.

Jude Underwood had sat there in "the Office" a little while longer, slowly puffing on his pipe. He missed Annabel more than ever, but in any event he could not stay long. He searched with his equanimous grey-green eyes for the one security camera he knew must be there. His eyes rested upon the clear quartz paper-weight on the heavy, ornate desk. Wolfgang Mueller, he knew, must be watching him.

"Our fates are now entwined," he had commented, trying to contain a protective ferocity he had for Annabel, "on the other side of night."

Ships departed, dodging solar flares which finally consumed the Earth as a fire-ball, and it set behind them, as hot as at formation.

Now Wolfgang and Claudia Mueller were on the trail again. They had dodged quasars and black holes, passed unharmed through asteroid belts, and, now that they existed again a billion years hence, they would never give up. Revenge is not only sweet, it is necessary.

Wolfgang Mueller's brain was fully functional, and his mind was like a steel trap, but it had caught only worms. His mind was full of worms. Claudia Mueller was venal as they get. The only people they got along with were each other. He was a man possessed by rage, and she a woman vicious. The Big Crunch only made them worse.

The only two smarter were Jude Underwood and Annabel Scrivenor. But that did not make them more powerful, nor necessarily more devious. Now the Big Crunch was over, and new life was dawning, but the old had not entirely died. It had been a tight race with gravity wells collapsing on all sides.

Annabel tried to console Lisbeth in the library with an antique parking meter. "You see, you put fifty dollars in and get a full hour."

"That's taxation without representation," Lisbeth pointed out, "plus I'm starving."

"Would you like ketchup on your burger?"

"My parents are dead. I'll have extra ketchup, please."

"We're your parents now. I'll also bring a milkshake."

Meanwhile, the pursuit was still hot. "Down and to the right," Jude predicted again.

"They won't escape!" repeated Wolfgang Mueller to Claudia.

Jude Underwood, Annabel Scrivenor, and Lisbeth Elkhorn had overcome the Big Crunch. But it was not the fatal end.

The king with his executor were appearing before parlaiment with the kings friend, the chimpanzee Baboo, and a few crows.

"We are on the brink of a new era," the king announced.

Baboo signed, "Remember well."

"We have," the king continued, "no official administrative oversight body that adequately addresses my concerns." Baboo puffed on a cigarette, with a luxurious exhale. The king momentarily watched a plume of smoke drift up to the hanging gardens above, which made the parlaiment hall seem covered by a jungle canopy. The king went on: "I am assigning Baboo here to be my special laiason, towards the end of character analysis should our planet, as I fully expect, be met with the challenges of strangers in our midst. I shall report post-haste to the press for us to be on alert for the unusual." A crow alighted upon the kings shoulder, but said nothing. This silence deepened the kings concern further. Baboo immediately signed that this special session was closed. Parlaiment, the wisest men and women of their age, dispersed with consternation, and some dismay, and even dread. Their peaceful home must now confront the new revelations of people from the stars, and expect the unexpected, the unwelcome guests and their vagaries. At least, they knew, in Baboo they had their finest representative.

The king decided to abdicate in favor of Baboo. On Chapel Hill a grand coronation occured, and the king proudly placed the jewel-encrusted golden crown on Baboo's head. "The honor is mine and his," Baboo the chimpanzee signed, and then he decided to retire into meditation and a cigarette, and speaking to more crows. Crows were always useful friends, Baboo knew full well. There tended to be many clans of crows wandering the royal palace. After some consideration, the chimpanzee took his first seating in the throne room, to hear supplicants. The most severe matter was that a young boy had cheated on an exam. Fianlly, Babboo retreated for further meditation.

"We can only hope and pray," Jude Underwood whispered to Annabel and Lisbeth as they raced from their nemesis. It was his actions with Sebastion and Stefan Mueller that had made possible the inclusion of Lisbeth on a ship. That part had gone according to plan. But now they must survive the consequences of enduring wrath and enmity. As the galaxies spread out again, reformed only a billion years ago, Jude knew without a shadow of a doubt where to go. The M-class planet of the new Atlantis was their only hope. They could race and endure space only so long, it was a losing gambit. Already they had danced and dodged a thousand times , and it could only last to their advantage so long. Wolfgang and Claudia Mueller were not easily fooled. Traces and trails would remain.

Baboo signed to his old friend, the former king. "Trouble comes to the garden," he said.

"Which garden? Our planet, or the Royal Botanical Gardens?"

"Both," Baboo signed.

"These are grave matters, indeed."

Wolfgang and Claudia Mueller were hell-bent on vengeance. Their quest was burning embers of hatred. But not because they loved their twin sons, Sebastian and Stefan. That was not in their nature. They sought vengeance because they had lost power, the power to alter humankinds destiny, and make themselves the sole survivors. Now their enmity was turned to Jude Underwood and Annabel Scrivenor, their goal to survive the rest of the race. They did not know, however, of the existence of Lisbeth Elkhorn. But if they would find out, their murderous frenzy would only increase.

The tumult of the universe had once blackened the sky. But they had personal anger to match.

Lisbeth sat reading an old book, Dickens stories of children. She wondered what it would be like to meet one.

The twin ships, like Cain pursuing Abel, shot through an asteroid belt, reversed propulson, and splashed down into a churning ocean. There velocity was tamed, but events were to speed up.

Jude Underwood manipulated the trios craft as swiftly as the water would allow, and found the grand river that would lead to River City where the Royal Palace lay. Jude focussed with the deepest part of his brain, and Lisbeth Elkhorn was deposited in the Royal Botanical Gardens, waking up from her reading among the topiaries and fruit trees. Baboo the king was waiting, reflectively smoking a cigarette.

"Ooh," said Lisbeth, "are you a child?"

The chimpanzee signed, "At heart," but Lisbeth could not understand.

The former king emerged from viewing the nasturtiums. "You will both go into seclusion now," and he lead them by the hands away from the garden. The crows were commenting furiously.

Jude Underwood and Annabel Scrivenor arrived in the garden mere seconds before their pursuers, dressed in defensive vestments and with lasers at the ready.

The Mueller's appeared, likewise appointed. They were not as smart, but their viciousness made them more cunning.

"Lay down your arms," tried Jude, "and we shall forgive, and forget mortality."

"Your words are empty, and far too late," replied Claudia Mueller, staking out the showdown the Mueller's considered inevitable. She went straight after Jude, and Wolfgang chose Annabel. The battle would be swift, as lasers flickered and flashed in the gathering dusk. The crows were in an uproar.

"Do not risk your lives," Jude objected.

"We obey the code," Claudia returned. "Might makes right, from the beginning."

"You're deluded," Jude said in fear.

"We are the human race!" Claudia cried. Jude could not follow her lasers. One passed through his armor and penetrated his very heart.

"I love you," he said to Annabel, without another breath.

Annabel faced the Mueller's nearly overcome with grief, even as she tried to be mindful of her own predicament. She would seek Lisbeth. She concentrated with the deepest part of her brain, and disappeared.

"We are victorious!" Wolfgang Mueller declared triumphantly over the corpse. His wife Claudia turned to him and beheaded him with one of her lasers.

"You fool for never suspecting!" She detracted her lasers and proceeded to wander for seclusion amidst the topiaries. The crows took flight, speaking loudly to one another. A raven alighted near the flesh, but would touch neither the good nor the evil.

It took hours for Annabel to find Lisbeth, who sat disconsolately behind a network of security labyrinths.

The former king spoke through an electronic translator. "Baboo says he likes you," said the former king. "He says, let us live for the small things, and forget about the great." The 15-year-old Lisbeth felt comforted, and lit the chimpanzees cigarette.

"I am an orphan," she explained, "and now I have been separated from my foster family."

"We are your new family, Baboo says," the former king responded with sympathy. A raven had been allowed through the labyrinth, and alighted on Baboo's shoulder. At this, the former king began to shed a tear. "We shall do everything within our power," the former king swore, "to keep you hidden forever." But forever was a long time.

Annabel Scrivenor finally reached Lisbeth and Baboo as they sat in their isolation. She hugged Lisbeth, but she herself was inconsolable. Annabel eulogized Jude:

"A most terrible mourning and grief,
Consumes as fire to a leaf,
As courageous love arrives too late,
To save itself against the hate,
That steals forth boldly as a thief.

My one true love ended far too soon,
Like sun and stars and brilliant moon,
It set, and made itself another place,

Jeremy Balfour

Buried in the earth far from the face
Of the hopes of April, May, and June.

The universe is reeling, mad,
There were a million kisses yet to be had.
Agree: we must make a new start,
To find our place in love with heart,
As on his grave decaying flowers, sad,

Remind me of the days, most glad,
When one sweet touch was all we knew,
Forgetfull, all, of the turning of the screw,
And I shall remember him as a lad,
As fine as the brightest apple, as true as Galahad,
Who with fate had to grapple,
Now love knows good from bad:
Sorrow rules the darksome day,
That said love must leave, and the void must stay.
This you only know when love goes away."

Lisbeth added:

"Now has come December,
The year, once love, is now decay,
Yet always we shall remember
The merry month of May,
Which shone with bright rain showers, then sun,
While winters silent grey has come,
With alarm, a scene of powers,
Which shall make the rivers run
Through untold length of hours,
Meeting, like the one,

Who has seen the grace of towers,

Tasted sweets and sours,

As though a garden growing from."

Baboo signed his appreciation with a winsome applause.

The people commented in secret horror as Claudia Mueller drifted through the marketplace. But it was illegal to take any life. Yet many things were noted: the enmity of her purple eyes, the cruel lines about them, and the single crease upon her brow. She was allowed to pass, but would continue to be observed. Her rumor spread out about her like a stalking terror. And indeed, this she was. In her ferocity, she deeply relished the events of the botanical gardens. Her next mission would perhaps prove more difficult: find and destroy Annabel Scrivenor, and be the last (she thought) of the race. She still did not know of the existence of Lisbeth Elkhorn.

The crows croaked and cawed about River City. Claudia Mueller took up free residence at the Silver Temple. Crows took flight to the royal palace.

Annabel Scrivenor was unconsolable, even by Lisbeth, and felt deathly ill. The denial of love was making her waste away, as it sometimes does. Jude Underwood had said many times, "If I die first, do not despair. Despair is an immortal enemy, and we are all mortals, yet renew: all good things may return." But she had lost all her optimism, and her will to live. She passed away in her sleep one night.

Lisbeth could barely endure the grief herself. Yet she knew light would dawn on a new day, her young heart, with resiliency learned from many lost loves, could still recover. But she eulogized sweet Annabel:

"I remember, I remember,
When life was seeming fair,
And the world of childhood quiet passed,
With never so much as a care.
Now I grieve, for I take my leave,
Of Annabel, sweet Annabel,
And remember the Dragon in its lair,
His eyes a darksome spell, a stare.

'She was a child, and I was a child,'
Yet we moved through time fraught with fate,
And tumult to the mild.
She none could save, and over her grave,
Tremble leaves in the shining air,
I take this time to share,
As deciding stars tear down the bars,
And time itself doth wear."

Lisbeth Elkhorn was learning Baboo's sign language, with the help of the former king. "Time is our most precious commodity," signed the chimpanzee, then paused momentarily to reflectively puff away on a cigarette. It eased his nervous tension: he was desperately protective of this young teenager. The former king sat morosely, contemplating suicide. Lisbeth and Baboo decided to dance with each other, far from the cares of their world. The old king enjoyed a few minutes of mirth.

Baboo followed a suggestion by Lisbeth and tried his hand at poetry with finger-paints:

"For all that you hold dear,
To all those who have ears to hear:
Live life fulfilled,
Afore the time your candle's stilled
And one thing never go near:

Death! Sudden, ye be killed,
The one thing to make us live that we most fear.
Waste not! But find the course,
Never the cart before the horse,
And never a horse-shoe upside-down,
But wear the luckiest smile and never a frown,
As sundry people mill,
About the sadness of the Town.

Let the stars rain down!
And never creep about the stair
To Heaven, for hell lies waiting there,
And unless you wear a seamless gown,
Ye shall not find a happy home,
But in twilight with no stars shall roam,
At best a ghost that wanders in the gloam.
You have put the cart before the mare!
Hold dear this book, and every care!
For ye were a child once, come from the womb,
And happy or not shalt thou lie in a tomb:
The same from cradle to grave;
What lucky penny can you save?
But love, which shall die too soon."

Claudia Mueller sat in a pew of the Silver Temple, writing: "Time must have its stop, and Death conquer all. Already lies the staircase, up from Babel to future doom. There are no words for the wise, to conquer death. Only an inhale and exhale of poisonous breath, the kneeding of the soul like a bread with no oven, but the bitter flames of hell. In the end, "la finis," as sure as the shark to the fish. Life is circumscribed all 'round by death, life slips through the most powerful grasp, a mere plaything for a child, that will destroy his own toy before the next Christmas. The saints went marching in, now all lie 'neath mossy bed. They suffered their trials and now are better off dead. There is no knowing where life will lead, except in the end a futile hour of need."

Lisbeth Elkhorn appeared, informed by a crow, before the massive ornate altar of jade and turquoise. She sat next to Claudia Mueller. Neither could move, as if time itself was frozen. Yet Claudia Mueller's purple eyes glowed with envy, and yet a secret delight. The crease in her brow deepened.

Finally, they could speak.

"I come for vengeance," Mrs. Mueller stated first. She was nearly squirming with greed for this new victim.

"I am vengeance," stated Lisbeth. They contemplated each other with extreme distaste and loathing, but could not move. Time itself came to a halt.

"I have here a gift for you," Claudia broke the silent spell, thinking only of the dagger she had in her sheath.

Lisbeth sensed this, and struggled against time. The two remaining members of the race were inextricably bound to each other by the slow torment of venqeance and its creed.

Lisbeth, too, had a dagger, poisoned with curari, just in case. She looked at Death straight in its purple eyes, purple as Karpozy's Sarcoma.

"There is only one cause in this universe, and that is life," Lisbeth Elkhorn enunciated, nearly weeping over her losses. Time began to move again, and she swiftly put her dagger into Mrs. Mueller's left eye. Claudia let out a terrible groan of agony. Time, it turned out, was on the side of life, not death. Claudia's eye dribbled down her face, but with the poison coursing through her veins she yet moved, and fled to the steeple of the Silver Temple.

Lisbeth pursued. "It is the hour of children everywhere!" she cried.

"Curse you, and God!" came the bitter reply. "Follow me at your life's peril!"

Claudia Mueller was yet swift, and undaunted by her injury. Her one good eye guided her upwards, reaching for the sky like the Tower of Babel. Lisbeth was close behind, as the spiral staircase, growing narrower, drove the pair onwards to an ultimate finality. They reached the bell of the tower simultaneously, even as it was tolling twelve.

Claudia slashed with her own dagger at Lisbeth's eyes, and had a vengeance with a blow to one, but she began to be weakened by the curari. Lisbeth, a child not yet grown, had the final word: "Hell calls hell," she cried above the tolling of the bell, and struck Claudia Mueller's other glowing, purple eye. Her eyes dribbled forth. Her mind, however, was yet full of worms, and would not cease. Lisbeth pushed Claudia neatly from the bell-tower, with its final gong, and down she plummeted, as though an end to the confusion of tongues. The crows peered in silent satisfaction, in the otherwise deserted street below. Lisbeth had conquered death, despite her eye, and was now free to grow up.

Lisbeth Elkhorn reached her twenty-first birthday, lucky twenty-one, and was coronated High Priestess of the realm, the vision in her one good eye quite clear. Later, back in the Royal Botanical Gardens, growing peacefully, Lisbeth read her most recent work to her dear friend Baboo the king, friends for life:

"Although I have grown,
And live perched on high,
What I never have known,
Is the sweet by-and-by,
For others have shown
My reason to cry:
Friends come and go, and I never know why.

But may I say this, at least:
Love best you can, as if it a feast,
For no matter how you try,
Death comes stalking like a beast,
Ending love with barely a sigh.
I can see this with only one eye."

Lisbeth Elkhorn was all grown up, as she remembered, even so, her childhood tears. Now her one good eye would never dim.

"We see you as you are," Baboo the chimpanzee signed. "A friend for life."

The crows cawed in approval, and the two of them laughed. Through the tears, laughter.

CHAPTER NINETEEN:
A Meeting Down the Midway

Thaddeus had not looked out the window of his humble inn yet. He had been absorbed in deep prayer and reflection for many hours, taken some unleavened bread with a sip of wine, and then, for some reason unknown to him, had decided to sweep before he left.

The morning was breaking upon the town, and the light shown in bars through the wooden shutters. Thaddeus, still with a tear in his eye, approached and thrust open the shutters, and peered with consternation and doubt upon a sky of clouds tinged with pink and green by the morning light.

The city was beginning to bustle beneath his window, the same city that has sealed Yeheshua's fate: there were food-vendors, and smithies, and candle-makers, and palmists. This was the same city, the city of judgement.

It was the fourth day. Mary Magdalena had told the gathered apostles of her sighting, yet how could they believe? Some had said He would arise after three days, some said He sat in Heaven on the right hand of God with the thieves He was crucified with, but Matthew had said that Judas had locked Him in a wooden tower on the Sea of Galilee, to question Him there as to His ministry and preaching. But Judas was missing to answer, and

Yeheshua. They were left only with a ragged faith, except Mary, who was insistent.

Duty called. Thaddeus removed himself from the window and packed his light satchel, and finished the wine. He was to meet Bartholomew by the north gate of the city as arranged, to journey north on the road to Armenia, to spread the faith and then settle. Paul would go to Rome. Thomas the Doubter would take Mary Magdalene in the direction of India, and finally settle there in Kerala. Age would not catch up on them all until their missions were fulfilled.

For now, there would be but little bread upon the road. Thaddeus tipped the innkeeper a bare minimum, yet this did not concern the innkeeper in the little. Rather, he was just sad to see such a group of friends leaving his auspices. He leaned over the check-out counter to Thaddeus, and said, "All good things shall come to pass, all in good time." Thaddeus nodded a little in recognition, his badly injured faith finding an inkling of new hope. "You see," the innkeeper continued, "death is just the beginning..." Thaddeus shook his hand, the last to leave, that pink and green morning, and, throwning his satchel over his shoulder, went out to meet the day.

He was blinded by the light, and at first stumbled through the throng to find his way. Then the emptier alleyways preceded and in time he reached the north gate of Salem.

Bartholomew was there before him. Thaddeus found him squatting, conversing quietly with a blind beggar. "I have been blind for twenty years," the beggar spoke, "yet do I see, as sure as you hear my voice. The

Covenant of Levi is meant for those who do not see, who need salvation. Then their faith will be tested as to their belief in the Covenant."

"Tell me," Batholomew replied eagerly, as was his wont, "is the Kingdom of Heaven at hand?"

"Verily," quoth the beggar, "the Kingdom of Heaven is always at hand, it fills the streets like running rain, the valleys like slow-drifting fog, and covers the hills with a gentle drift of snow. For those who know the signs, the Kingdom of Heaven is at hand. There are wheels, and thrones, and chariots of fire in the sky..." he trailed off.

"Bartholomew, well met," hailed Thaddeus, gripping Bartholemew's arm and patting his back. "The road is long, we must away."

"There they are!" cried a toothless woman to a passing legionary. "They are one with the fake Messiah!"

"Be quiet, old woman," said the legionary, and laughed, "before I crucify you!"

"They have hubris before Caesar," another legionary put in, but no more was said, and Thaddeus and Bartholomew hastily departed Salem.

"I am not sorry to leave this place," said Thaddeus to Bartholomew.

"Did you not hear?" Bartholomew nearly sighed. "There are wheels and thrones and chariots of fire! The Kingdom is everywhere!"

The glaring sun evaporated the pink and green clouds into nothingness. They fasted during their slow-moving sojourn by day, and broke fast at the falling even-time. Bartholomew had brought bread with clotted cream, and olives. The evening star was dimmed by a great gibbous moon, and falling stars, like chariots of fire, broke the darkening sky. At last the moon set, and the evening star shown full. As they encamped by the side of the road, just these two apostles, now with a different mission, a holy man approached from the west, with a gift of pomegranates and figs for them.

They spoke kind words to the man, who was tall and clean-shaven, with short-cropped hair, like a Roman by evident seeming. Yet his Hebrew speech was stranger than that. The man pointed to the evening star as it set. "You will see, in the End, there is no God but God, and He is One," the man said. The two apostles nodded in rapt agreement. "Like the Light of the Eye which is One, all arises out of the one thing and then fades back into the One. The Light of the Body is the Light of the Eye. There is only That. Not two trees, but one."

But at this last Thaddeus was caught. "There must be two trees," he said as the man ended his recitation. "The Tree of Life and that of the Knowledge of Good and Evil."

"Yes, there are two trees," interjected Bartholomew, "even if the body is One."

The man stood up suddenly, and towered imperiously above the pair. He raised both his arms, and the stars began moving all in different directions, phasing and crashing and flying. His body burned with fire. One green light in the sky began to burn greater and greater, until it hung over the three in near-blinding radiance. The man was gone, and the green light meandered up into the night sky, even as the sky took familiar shape again.

Bartholomew was cringing upon the sod.

"Shalom, Bartholomew," Thaddeus urged. "Peace."
"There is only one Tree!" Bartholomew cried.

END

Jeremy Balfour

BIOGRAPHY

Jeremy Balfour (Mark Woods Browning) is a product of Berkeley, California. He was raised in a liberal society which still has a continuity. For thirty-two years Mark worked in private practice as a counselor and "life coach," utilizing Humanistic, Transpersonal, and Jungian psychology. He is a long-term student of Eastern and Western mysticism. Some of his other interests include not only science-fiction and rhyming verse, but sociology, political science, satire, and comic books. He has a dearly beloved adult son.